OWLHOOT BANDITS

When ex-Cavalry officer Lieutenant Bob McCleave hurries home to the Diamond M in Rockwall County, New Mexico, it's because his father's freight business is under threat. Approaching home, Bob clashes with freight raiders at Indian Ridge. But when it appears that it's the local banks that are now at risk, he becomes a temporary deputy. After a renegade outfit raids the South-Western National in Broad Creek, will Bob's ruthlessness and shooting accuracy be enough to overthrow those responsible?

DAVID BINGLEY

OWLHOOT BANDITS

Complete and Unabridged

LINFORD
Leicester

First published in Great Britain in 1970

First Linford Edition
published 2009

British Library CIP Data

Bingley, David
  Owlhoot bandits.—Large print ed.—
Linford western library
1. Western stories
2. Large type books
I. Title
823.9'14 [F]

ISBN 978–1–84782–544–5

Published by
F. A. Thorpe (Publishing)
Anstey, Leicestershire

Set by Words & Graphics Ltd.
Anstey, Leicestershire
Printed and bound in Great Britain by
T. J. International Ltd., Padstow, Cornwall

This book is printed on acid-free paper

1

The big dun horse sneezed on trail dust, shaking its head and rolling its neck. The dust-caked rider on its back clicked his tongue sympathetically. He leaned forward and gently ruffled the tousled mane, receiving a snicker of thanks in recognition.

The white blaze on the dun's head showed up boldly even in the brassy glare of early afternoon heat. Many men with two days of riding behind them would have found some shade and taken advantage of it at that time of the day, but this rider, Bob McCleave, was a restless young man not long out of the United States cavalry, and he was keen to complete his journey and make contact with his folks at the McCleave horse ranch and freighting station, known in the district as the Diamond M.

The two days' ride had brought ex-Lieutenant McCleave all the way from Fort Verne, over the North Texas border and into New Mexico territory's Rockwall County, east of the Pecos river. In his keenness to get home quickly, Bob had forsaken the more frequently used county trails and had ridden across broken country, some of it virgin soil, judging by the rock and earth which had passed under the shoes of his mount.

From time to time he whistled. His tunes were old marching songs and riding ditties well known to the cavalry. The music of men on horseback, which was usually accompanied by jingling bits and swinging saddle harness. A long time had elapsed since Bob last rode trails on his own.

The sun was punishing him. Every few minutes he pulled the red bandanna from his throat and mopped his lean, slightly square face with it. His hair was straight, thick, long and black. The brows above the strong curved nose were short and barred. The green eyes were clear and keen, half-closed against the sun's glare. A cream stetson decorated with a snakeskin band sat squarely on his compact head. Broad shoulders in a dun shirt with buttoned pockets appeared too large for his slim waist and the long legs which were encased in new denim levis. He was six feet tall in his cowhide boots.

Mostly, his attention was focussed upon a ridge which crossed his line of ride about two miles up ahead.

'That there hogsback is Indian Ridge, Blaze,' he murmured conversationally to the horse. 'You ain't seen it before, but it sure does hold an important place in my memory.'

Five years with the cavalry had kept him active in Arizona and then in Texas, but never had he been called upon to serve in New Mexico territory. He was returning after sixty months' absence from Rockwall County, apart from a short furlough about three years earlier.

As a child he had swarmed all over

Indian Ridge with boys of his own age. They had had climbing races with worn moccasins on their feet, and, later, on surefooted ponies they had sought and found circuitous routes to the top which a quadruped could take, though they had never told their fathers that they had ridden their mounts up the ridge, in case it was ruled out as being too risky.

Not many men knew the ridge as well as Bob McCleave. He was approaching it from the opposite side to the one he knew best. His mouth quirked in a wry smile as he reflected that it was not really on his most direct route to the Diamond M. He was about to climb it because of the view from the top. From an eminence a little to the north of the central cleft one could see the home buildings of the Diamond M through a gap in the hills to the north-west.

At the foot of the ridge, the dun was permitted a ten minute break, during which Bob slackened the saddle girth and also rubbed it down with bunch grass.

The route up the east side was a zigzag, and much narrower most of the way than the paths on the other side. On the steeper parts of the path he walked the sweating animal, but on others he coaxed and bullied it along, and approved of the way in which it stood up to the exacting test.

It was blowing hard when the nearest part of the cleft came into sight, and yet it increased speed as the gradient levelled out. Three minutes later, horse and man emerged on the west side and further progress was stopped. Bob concentrated on getting the salt perspiration out of his eyes before he sampled the view before him.

His ears were busy while his hands did the job. Fast approaching the part of the trail which flanked the ridge on the west side were two wagons. Four horses pulled each of them, and scarcely twenty yards showed between the tailgate of the first and the lead horses of the second.

The wagons were heavy freighters, and, consequently, their wheels put up a good deal of dust as they left their marks on the trail. Bob was not surprised when his straining eyes picked out the writing on the canvas sides of the vehicles. Each of them had painted in bold letters *McCleave Freighting Company*, and a diamond shape had been daubed around the first letter of the name.

Bob smiled to himself as he fumbled out his spyglass, intent upon seeing the features of the driver of the lead wagon. Before he could get the glass to his eye, however, the unexpected happened. Three bright red flashes occurred along the tops of rocks some fifty yards above the other side of the trail. Bullets ripped into the dust ten yards ahead of the first wagon's team.

The driver, an elderly man, rose to his feet on the box and peered in the direction of the attack. His mouth opened and closed a couple of times before he made up his mind what to do. He cracked his whip and attempted to keep his team moving speedily forward.

The driver of the second wagon reacted in the same way, but a second flurry of bullets spooked the lead horses again, and in a flash the old driver was fighting for control. His wagon rocked to a stop, two horses striving to turn and two wanting to go on. In spite of its load, the freighter rocked. The driver's angry cries were drowned by more shots and the frantic whinnying of the horses.

Bob's jaw tightened in anger. He had heard reports that his father's freight had suffered once or twice, but he had not felt any great anxiety due to the knowledge, having thought that casual thieves had made the earlier strikes; now he was not sure. As he watched and tried to decide what was best to be done, the drivers braked their vehicles and went for their guns.

Bullets from the rocks tore into the canvas. The action looked very much a one-sided affair with no one either way, up or down the trail, to take a hand on the wagoners' behalf. Bob studied the route down the ridge side. It was much the same as he had always known it. Precipitous at the turns, but not at all deadly, provided the adventurer took his time. He had ridden down it before, on the back of a surefooted pony. He could have done with that pony on this occasion, or one of the mules on the Diamond M horse ranch.

The dun was steaming and shifting fretfully, at once tired and disturbed by the gunfire at the lower level.

A patch of canvas smouldered on the second wagon. A man shouted in anger and threw water on it from the inside. This sufficed to kill the blaze. It also goaded Bob into delayed action. Pulling his Winchester from the saddle scabbard, he put it to his shoulder and fired three bullets towards the rocks on the other side.

His work added to the reverberations, and caused a brief pause in the exchanges as both sides looked round to find the source of the latest-comer to the shooting. He chose that moment to send the dun down the first leg of the staggered path. For twenty yards it fought the rowels. Then it gathered momentum, and for several more yards it was almost at a gallop. Fear, and Bobs efforts to slow it, finally made it dig in its hooves some five yards from the first turn.

In a flurry of dust and soil, its fore hooves came to a standstill and the rider's flapping stomach returned to its normal position. The first angry shot from the other side winged its way towards him. As a result of the dun's precipitate move, three small rocks detached themselves from the hillside and rolled down the slope, gathering others as they went along, and starting a minor landslide.

The slide continued all the way to the trail level, and stones bounced around the wheels of the first vehicle. Again, there was a lull in the firing. A minute went by and then the attackers redoubled their efforts as three riders came out from the rocks on the west side of the trail and pumped shells at the wagons from the cover of boulders which sheltered them to shoulder height.

Meanwhile, Bob half-turned, half-jumped his dun around the first hairpin bend and came on apace down the second leg of the descent. The second bend was negotiated much more carefully, although one gunman was concentrating his attention on the descending rider and getting much closer in his efforts to wing him.

Bob paused long enough to send two more shots into the boulders where the mounted riders had appeared. One bullet ricochetted and caused concern for the trio. The three riders moved their position, riding further north behind the scattered boulder cover and attacking instead the second wagon.

Excitement and weariness affected the dun's performance. All went well in the terrifying descent until the last fifty feet. There, half way along a stony path, rendered more difficult by protruding roots, the dun found its way barred by a recently-fallen rock. Too late, it tried to position itself to leap the rock. In slithering to a halt just short of it, the poor animal lost its balance and had to make a leap sideways.

Seconds later, Bob parted company with the dun, hurtling away from it in a dead drop which made his heart thump. The horse bounced in a patch of thick dry brushwood, and went on down with its legs flailing the air. At the same time, Bob dropped feet first into a narrow niche between two large rocks at trail level. The landing jarred his legs, although there was soft soil and some fern beneath his feet. He straightened up very cautiously, assured himself that no bones were broken and found that his hat was no longer on his head.

Only about four feet of rock was above him. Moreover, there was a crack in the rock at waist level which would enable him to extricate himself without difficulty. Counting himself very lucky, he began the ascent. His single right-handed Colt and holster dug into his thigh as he climbed, but he was glad that the weapon had not left him.

A slight breeze tousled his hair as his head cautiously came into view. The firing had almost stopped. Only the old man in the first wagon occasionally tried a shot from the tailgate. The three raiders, with faces masked, were breaking out of cover and heading for the second wagon, full of confidence.

As they came, one of the riders called: 'Any signs of that jasper who fired at us from the ridge?'

'Didn't you see him do his death leap? He's buried somewhere at the back of that trailside rock. You don't need to pay any attention to him any more.' This statement was accompanied by a coarse laugh from a barrel chest.

Bob took in the scene, and heard some of the shouted conversation. The first raider was ahead of the second wagon, waving a brace of six guns towards the first freighter. The second man, the one with the coarse laugh, was peering over a spotted bandana at the empty box of the second vehicle. The third man was cautiously edging up to the rear of wagon number two. He looked to be a little on the jumpy side.

In a second, Bob had his Colt resting on the top of the rock. He selected as his first target the second man in the spotted bandanna. In these circumstances, he figured the raiders did not deserve any warning as to their plight. He fired two bullets in quick succession. The barrel chest received both of them, and while Bob was lining up on the first man, his earlier victim slipped limply out of the saddle and hit the trail, being dead already.

The raider's leader swung his mount about in a spectacular attempt to get into cover, but by that time the veteran driver of the first wagon had opened up on him from the ground, having crawled under the box. Although the firing from the rocks on the west side was resumed, Bob's timely shooting was having its effect.

The driver spooked the horse and Bob grooved the leader across the belly before the latter withdrew. The third man did not wait for instructions, but turned his mount about and retreated into the rocks from which he had arrived.

Very cautiously, Bob crawled out on the hot flat top of his rock and peered around.

'Howdy, young fellow!' the driver called. 'If he weren't away in the cavalry I'd say you had to be young Bob McCleave come home at a mighty fine time!'

The old driver stuck his head out between the wheels and grinned, showing yellow gapped teeth in a face the colour of mahogany. He pulled off his straw hat and scratched his head of stiff white hair, cut short like a brush.

'Well I'll be darned,' Bob called in return, 'if it ain't old Dan Rees, lookin' jest as old an' as fit as ever! How about the boys in the other wagon? Are they all right?'

'I guess so,' Rees surmised. 'As like as not they ran out of ammunition, or somesuch. I never could get that boy of mine to take these here jobs seriously.'

As Bob was climbing down to trail level, the voice of Willie Rees, Dan's thirty-nine year old son, came from the depths of the other wagon. 'Pa, I got me a slight groove in an awkward place for shootin' an' old Uncle Pete, here, has run out of ammunition, can you beat that?'

Dan emerged, scrambled to his feet. 'Go get that hoss of yours, young Bob. We'll wait here till you get back. I don't figure them masked boys will be along this way again in a hurry. You sure did scare them off!'

Bob hesitated and then took Dan's advice. He came back ten minutes later with the dun in tow. By a miracle it had suffered no lasting injuries. Nearing the spot where the two wagons were

15

resting, he heard the voices of the crews raised in excited speculation.

Dan was saying: 'If you two ask me, I'd say that insurance fellow in the town is jest as interested in seein' folks robbed as protected against outlaws!'

Willie Rees, his arm in a sling, laughed raucously. 'You ain't still thinkin' Curly Thomas got as far as the insurer with Mr McCleave's money, are you? Don't you believe it, Pa. I feel it in my bones that Curly's skipped with the money!'

Bob was a little baffled by this conjecture, but he had expected things to be different after an absence of five years. He wondered *how* different they were going to prove.

2

The withdrawal of the two surviving renegades marked the end of the shooting from the rocks. The freight men and Bob were left to study the unfamiliar face of the florid, bald-headed man who had worn the spotted mask. The low-barrelled bay horse which had carried him bore no distinguishing marks. The renegade was a complete stranger.

Bob took it upon himself to search the area from which the attack had been launched. He found the exact location of the marksmen, but that was all. They had pulled out smoothly and efficiently, as though at a prearranged signal. No one had held back to investigate the fate of Spotted Mask.

The sound of hooves from a new direction dissuaded the young man from trying to follow the trail of the withdrawing outlaws. Instead, he worked his way through the trailside rocks back to the track, and satisfied his curiosity about the latest-comers.

He found four horse drovers from his father's home ranch, on their way to the county seat, Broad Creek, which was a few miles further south. All four showed surprise when old Dan Rees told them what had happened. Nathan Mallin, who was in charge of the four men and twelve horses, listened with his small mouth pursed, all the while stroking his lantern jaw.

At length, Dan grew tired of talking and paused to quench his thirst.

'How would it be if the boys an' me escort you into Broad Creek?' Mallin suggested, his thin brows lifting.

Rees accepted with alacrity. This pleased Bob, because it left him free to hurry home and appraise his father of the latest development without laying himself open to criticism for leaving the wagons unprotected.

Forty minutes later, the high-stepping dun was in the last furlong of the journey which had started some fifty hours earlier. It jogged along the downgrade towards the cluster of home buildings and the sights and smells of a small but thriving community.

The main building was a long low rambling ranch house with galleries at the back and front. The shutters had recently been painted green, and this gave the scene a splash of colour which the bright sun failed to neutralize.

Flanking it on the north side was a series of buildings running west to east. First the smithy, the domain of Bill Read, the husband of Bob's eldest sister. Then a barn, a shed and the cookhouse. The shed was currently in use as an office, and presided over by Gunther Smith, who had married Art McCleave's younger daughter. At the west end there was a pair of stables, and in a matching position to eastward was the bunkhouse belonging to the hands.

Arthur McCleave's shock of white

hair and his intense blue shirt provided a focal point for Bob's eyes as he slowed for the paddock gate. McCleave Senior had been fifty when Bob went in the army. Now, he was fiftyfive. A little more stooped and heavier in the paunch. He suffered from rheumatism in the hip all the year round now, but his eyesight was as good as it had been thirty years ago. He recognized Bob at the first glance, and rose to his feet, awaiting his arrival.

Bob walked the dun across the yard as two or three old hands doing everyday chores came out into the open and noticed him. He gave them a ready smile and touched his hat, but his eyes were never long away from his father's face. Art's wife had died a few months before Bob left home. Now, he would be used to the life of a widower. Bob wondered how it suited him.

'Leave that hoss down by the rail, son, an' come on up here. It's good to see you.'

The meeting was a warm one with a

firm handshake and a mutual thumping on the back. They had only been seated five minutes when a Mexican woman came from the back of the house and placed a tray of coffee utensils in front of them. Bob did the pouring out, while Arthur listened to the details of the earlier part of the journey.

At the first mention of trouble to the two freighters on their way from Rockwall to Broad Creek the freight boss sat forward on the edge of his chair. Bob broadened out the story of the attack, after assuring his father that no serious harm had come to the crews or the stores.

Eventually, Bob had told it all. Arthur was stretched out at full length in his wicker chair, frowning at a cobweb in the ceiling above him, and looking far from pleased.

'Pa, I heard things from the Rees family which puzzled me. There was talk about an insurer in town who might be crooked. An' Willie said somebody called Curly Thomas might have skipped with some insurance money. How about explainin' these things to me? After dinner it might be more difficult, with the family around us an' the kids.'

The older man's mobile features showed traces of an inner turbulence before he began the explanation. He glared into an empty coffee cup as though it offended him.

'You never knew Curly Thomas. He came around about eighteen months ago. I took him on although he was more used to towns than to ranches. I felt he would be of use to me as a go between. You know I never go into towns unless I'm absolutely forced.'

'A man runnin' a freight line like you do, Pa, can't expect to prosper unless he shows himself now and again,' Bob observed quietly.

'It's too late to teach an old dog new tricks,' Arthur replied. 'Anyways, on two occasions unknown strangers held up my wagons, an' occasionally we heard rumours that strikes against freighters might get worse. So, when this hombre, Wilson Hargrove, set up in town as an insurer, I thought I'd test him out. I sent Curly to town to draw money from the bank and insure deliveries between Rockwall an' Broad Creek.'

'An' did Curly do the insurin'?' Bob persisted.

'I don't know, son. A week has gone by, an' Curly's not been back. We've known him go on a short drinkin' spree before this, but he's never absented himself for so long. I'm beginnin' to think he's moved on to new pastures.'

After a few seconds of silence, Bob resumed. 'After breakfast tomorrow, I'll go along to the county seat an' look into this insurin' business. You'd better give me a description of your man, Curly.'

Old Arthur noted the authority in his son's voice. He approved of it, and gave the required information.

★ ★ ★

Half an hour later, father and son went into the house to have a reunion with the rest of the family.

Jennie, the older daughter, a square-faced woman of thirty-four with a dominating personality, presided over the house. She prompted a conversation between Bob and her blacksmith husband, Bill Read. Bill was a shy, muscular man of thirty-five with thinning brown hair and a self-effacing manner. He kept backing away and pushing forward their twelve year old twins, Ricky and Rose.

Patricia, the other daughter, came into the main room with her bespectacled accountant husband, Gunther Smith, and their slim, leggy ten year old daughter, Maria, who was growing into something of a beauty. Patricia's talents ran mostly to cooking and dressmaking. She was a gentle, more tactful person than her older sister, and she often betrayed a sensitivity which was denied to Jennie.

All of them were keen to have Bob back in their midst, and the men in particular were keen to hear of his exploits with the cavalry. After the meal, the assembled kin showed signs of surprise when Bob intimated that he was riding for town on the following day. Already they had heard rumours of the setback on the main trail south, and they all assumed that Bob's visit had to do with the shooting incident and Curly Thomas.

The county seat, Broad Creek, was built with its thoroughfares on a square basis with the stone county courthouse in the middle. Its population had been slowly rising over the past decade. The recent arrival of an insurer was looked upon by some people as a sign that the inhabitants of the town were prosperous and forward looking.

Bob McCleave found the office of Wilson Hargrove, insurer, in a single room of an office block on Second Street. The lower half of the broad glass window had been painted green, but Bob could see over the painted portion by simply raising his head an inch or so.

Hargrove was sitting in the middle of his little domain with a battered coffee mug to hand, and a newspaper unfolded in front of him on the scarred desk. Behind him, on a hat rack, was a derby and a gret cutaway coat. He had a long thin face and nose accentuated by greasy black hair worn long and brushed down flat at the sides and the nape of the neck. From time to time he flicked his long drooping moustache with a horny thumb nail, or made slight adjustments to the brown buttoned vest which topped his soiled white shirt.

Presently, he frowned, and glanced up in the direction of the window. He saw Bob for the first time, and his grey eyes hardened. A hand dropped to the Colt at his right hip. The expression on the lugubrious face softened with an effort of will. The hand on the gun butt came away and gestured for the new arrival to step indoors.

Bob did so with alacrity, crossing the floor and shaking hands before dropping into the visitor's seat and eyeing up the fittings from there. Apart from the desk and the hat stand, there were two chairs and a wooden filing cabinet. Notices giving some details of the insurance services offered were pinned to the rear wall, and one paper intimated that Wilson Hargrove had the approval of Willis and Jason, the foremost insurers in New Mexico territory.

'What can I do for you, mister?'

Bob gave his name and explained how he came to be acting on behalf of his father, since his recent return to the ranch. He went on: 'Mr Hargrove, I'd like to ask you if a man named Curly Thomas ever came along to see you about insuring my father's freights between Rockwall and Broad Creek. What's your answer?'

Hargrove was slowly shaking his head. He appeared to be slightly embarrassed. 'This character, Curly Thomas, certainly has been in town, but he never came along here to insure any McCleave property, Bob. As a matter of fact, many of the townsfolk could confirm that Thomas was spendin' freely, if you ask around. But insurin', no. I kind of had the feelin' your father was not interested in my sort of business.'

Bob nodded. He requested permission to roll a smoke. When he had lit it, he resumed. 'My father gave him instructions to come along to you and insure freights between the two towns I mentioned. We're a little anxious about this state of affairs, especially since Curly hasn't been back to the ranch, an' since Pa's wagons were fired upon yesterday on the way to this town.'

'It's all about town, Bob,' Hargrove suggested. 'Accordin' to the way we have the facts, you happened along jest at the crucial time an' quite by accident. You acted as a kind of insurance for your Pa, who must otherwise have lost his cargoes, I fancy.'

Bob stood up and peered through the window into the street. He intimated that Hargrove would probably hear further from the Diamond M, and then left the office, heading for the bank to talk with the cashier who had furnished Thomas with the money. On the sidewalk opposite to the bank, three men were peering at a rectangle of canvas on an easel. Curiosity drew Bob to take a look at it. He found to his surprise that the artist, who was not present, had painted in oils a very realistic facsimile of the bank's frontage and some of the detail on either side. The other onlookers would have liked to draw him into a discussion about it, but the missing man, Thomas, and the funds he had acquired at the bank were uppermost in his mind and making him impatient.

Leary Rice, the senior cashier, took him into the private office of the bank and put him in the client's chair, while he, himself, occupied the padded swivel of the manager, who was not present. Rice was a lean, nervous little man in his early forties, with thinning hair and eyes greatly magnified by gold-rimmed spectacles. He looked ill at ease in his stores suit, but his voice was calm enough when he explained.

'Mr Bob, the note was properly signed by your father, and you must know that he doesn't like anyone in town querying his instructions. I paid out the hundred dollars to Thomas, as the note said, and since then I've seen the fellow livin' it up on the proceeds. He hasn't been back to the ranch, has he?'

Bob admitted as much and asked if Rice could suggest where the rascally fellow had gone. The cashier became a little offhand.

'You could look out in the waste-lands, towards the lesser creek, if you like.'

'Don't you think I'll be able to find him?' Bob felt prompted to ask.

'Oh, you could find him, all right. But what good will it do if his eternal guitar-playin' gives him away? I don't think you're the kind to shoot him for what he's done, an' you certainly won't get back the hundred dollars because he'll have about run through it all. He only quit town yesterday, an' that's a fact.'

Bob elicited a few more facts from the angry bank cashier and then tactfully left the bank building. On the other side of the street, the artist had returned. He was a tall, fair, good-looking young man with a big cream stetson pushed back off a brow furrowed with concentration. He was actually working on the canvas; jabbing at it with a brush, while the .44 Colt at his left side rocked on his hip.

Bob studied him briefly, and then turned his attention to the dun, which was pawing the sidewalk. He was about to do his utmost to bring in Curly Thomas and have him answer for his crime of misappropriating Diamond M funds. It was about time that the McCleave image had a face lift in the district.

3

If and when casual wrongdoers in Broad Creek wanted time to cool off, it was almost certain that they would head for the unbroken ground in the region of the lesser creek. Consequently, Bob McCleave moved in that direction quietly confident that he would find the man he was searching for without much difficulty.

Half an hour's ride down one side of the creek brought him within earshot of a plaintive song sung by a soft tenor voice, and accompanied by a guitar played with some skill. For two or three minutes, while the dun walked nearer, Bob listened to the man-made sounds blending in with those of nature, and wondered what manner of man Curly Thomas really was.

Fifty yards further forward, the lesser creek barred his path and brought the dun to a halt with ears twitching. The animal sniffed the water and wondered whether they would head into it. Curly Thomas was on the further side. Profusely growing bushes and shrubs hid him. There was no knowing just how near he really was to the water's edge.

Bob cleared his throat and filled his lungs. He was sitting the horse between a pair of willow trees well filled out with foliage.

He called: 'Hey, you with the guitar, is your name Thomas?'

The singing stopped abruptly, and Bob waited expectantly. The voice sounded deeper in pitch than when its owner had been singing. It came from a thin stand of timber more than fifty yards away.

'Who wants to know?'

'Answer the question, if you ain't ashamed of your name! I'm Bob McCleave! You're overdue in makin' contact with the Diamond M!'

The unseen man laughed. Something

in the tone of his laughter suggested that he might be under the influence of strong liquor.

'All right, so my name is Curly Thomas, but it won't do you any good, soldier boy, because I ain't comin' back to the Diamond M, an' I ain't waitin' for you to come any closer! Do you get the message?'

'Thomas, you're a fool! You betrayed a trust, an' since you failed to insure McCleave property with the money entrusted to you two Diamond M wagons have been attacked! An' so help me, you're goin' to have to pay for your betrayal of my father's trust, even if you've spent all the money!'

After a few seconds pause, Thomas answered. 'Say, that's fightin' talk. I guess that's the soldier in you talkin'. Are you determined to cross that water to get me, mister?'

Bob was really angry by this time. By way of an answer he jumped the dun into the water and headed it directly across the creek. He had just pulled his

Winchester out of the scabbard to keep it dry when the first rifle bullet whistled over his head. He ducked, but much too late to have done himself any good. The second shot was much nearer and he saw quite clearly that Thomas was determined to prevent his crossing. This was the time for hasty action. A man on a horse swimming a river was in a bad position to return the fire of a man on dry land whom he could not see.

Muttering angrily to himself, Bob plunged into the water and came up alongside of the dun which was rolling its eyes and wondering what the next development might be. He did all he could to assure it that it had nothing to fear and to keep it swimming across in the same direction as before. The Winchester had to be hastily returned to the scabbard. It would not have been possible to swim and take evasive action while carrying a shoulder weapon.

A third bullet came within a foot of Bob's head. He took a deep breath and surface-dived under the water, leaving his hat behind to mark the spot. For several yards he pulled hard, and then he surfaced again. The dun had veered a little to the right, and it was masking his head from the direction of the earlier shooting.

The pressure on the swimmer's lungs was gradually easing when the next gunshot tensed him up again. He ducked at once, but came up after about thirty seconds with a distinct feeling that something in the strange situation had changed. Two more gunshots followed in quick succession, but no bullets came his way.

Several seconds elapsed before his thoughts got round to the truth. Curly Thomas was under fire, not himself. This was an abrupt turn around. If Thomas was in trouble, there was nothing to show whether the latest gunmen were also hostile to Bob, or not. Certainly any riders from the sheriff's office would not have opened up on a man wanted for such a small offence as Curly Thomas. After all, if he had been in an agreeable frame of mind he could have worked off his debt to the Diamond M in a few months. Bob had never really thought that his father would have Thomas jailed.

Bob sucked in air, he ducked his head, made a stroke downwards and swam as far as he could in the direction of the bank. When ferns and other thick growths obscured him he stayed on the surface and worked his way up the bank until he could relax and hold on with his hands. Some fifty yards away, the dun was succeeding in scrambling ashore at the second attempt. The atmosphere was devoid of gunfire now, but that did not mean that the menace of the guns had faded.

Bob was loath to show himself. He listened for any sort of attack on the riderless horse, but none came. As he crawled over the top of the bank, he heard horses again, and briefly the voices of two men. He stood up and positioned himself behind a thick bush, wondering if his presence was known to the men with the horses.

The tension built up and then slowly ebbed as the riders moved further away from the water. Bob methodically cleaned his wet gun, and then worked his way like an Indian in the direction of the dun. In mysterious circumstances it was not wise for a man to be separated from his mount.

He was anxious to know the full facts of the attack on Thomas, but the horse needed help first. He had forgotten to slacken the saddle before entering the water and the leather was uncomfortably tight around the animal's girth now. He slackened it, and rubbed down the hide with handfuls of grass.

The timber stand was ominously quiet. Only the half-hearted snicker of a nervous horse betokened a living person there as Bob walked the dun in the desired direction. Five yards in from the edge of the trees, Curly Thomas' crumpled body was draped round the bole of a tree. Beside him was a finely marked Spanish guitar with a bullet hole through the thickest part of the base.

In life, Thomas had been a tall, thickset individual with kinky brown hair, and a rubbery face which easily moved into an infectious grin. He had earned his living before appearing at the Diamond M as a carpenter and a musician. He had big artisan's hands. In his middle forties, his forehead had been unlined before the bullet holed it. Two other slugs had entered his chest and robbed the big hands of their cunning both with music and with tools.

Bob knelt beside him, bareheaded, and wondered how Thomas fitted into the scheme of things. So far as he knew, the dead man had not done anything to bring about his untimely murder. Misappropriation of a few dollars did not merit that, and no one known to Art McCleave would shoot a man to death in the name of the McCleaves.

Obviously, Thomas had other enemies. People, perhaps, whom he had wronged at an earlier date. Or maybe he had information which others feared he might divulge. If he had given his confidence to the McCleaves, what might that information have been? Did he know something about the raiders who had attacked McCleave wagons? Perhaps that had something to do with his death.

Bob stood up. He pulled his wet shirt off his back and wondered what he ought to do about the shooting. It hurt him when he recollected that he had entertained very harsh thoughts about the dead man. Now, he had to take him back into town, lifeless, and fit for nothing more than Boot Hill.

His ears told him that the killers were now some distance away. They had headed west, and that way led towards town. If they kept going in the same direction, it was possible to cross the creek by a wooden trestle bridge near town, or they could keep on going westward, missing Broad Creek; or they could turn south.

Ten minutes elapsed, during which time he managed to get the dead body forked over the nervous sorrel gelding, and he collected his cream stetson which had drifted ashore. After that, he mounted up and headed towards town, keeping on the south side of the creek. Some five minutes before he reached the bridge, he heard the drumming beat of horses' hooves going across it. It seemed likely that he was hearing the sounds of Thomas' killers, but he could not be sure.

* * *

Slim Burrows, the town marshal of Broad Creek, was a former drifter who had settled in the town and made a life for himself. He owed no favours to the moneyed people of the town, or the ranchers in the surrounding country. He styled himself as a self-made man and liked people to think that all and sundry would be treated by him in the same way, according to the dictates of the law.

As the nickname suggested, Slim was a lean wiry individual. He had a slight squint, which did not in any way spoil him as a marksman. His legs, bowed from birth, still gave him sturdy support in his thirty-seventh year.

The horses slowing at the rail outside his office drew him to the window, in time to see Bob McCleave tie up the dun and the sorrel gelding. The inert figure on the gelding did not pass unnoticed. Some twelve to fifteen men had seen it also, and they had followed the determined young McCleave towards the office, thinking — as he did not explain — that he had sought the man who had robbed his father and personally disposed of him in a gun showdown.

Marshal Burrows was of the same opinion, and he looked annoyed as he waited for Bob to enter the office. He stood with his weight on one foot and toyed with an unlit cigarette in the corner of his mouth. Bob was still looking damp and bedraggled as he came in. He took off his hat and nodded to the marshal, a person who was unknown to him before this day.

'You're Marshal Burrows. Howdy.'

'An' you're Bob McCleave. Heard tell you were seekin' Curly Thomas on your Pa's behalf, but I didn't expect you'd bring him back lifeless. How did it happen, huh?'

Bob shook his head. 'You're assumin' that I killed him, marshal, but I didn't. I went after him, sure enough, an' I could hear him playin' his guitar, but I didn't shoot him. That was the work of two or three other men I never set eyes on.

'Thomas fired on me to try an' stop me crossin' the creek. While I was separated from my hoss an' actually swimmin' some other folks started shootin' at him. He had the three bullet holes in him when I found him on the ground among the some trees.'

'You didn't see the killers, an' you don't know who they were?'

'That's about the size of things. I heard folks ridin' ahead of me towards the bridge, but I couldn't say for sure that they came over it and into town. Thomas must have had some other enemies than the McCleave family. If you have any doubts about what I've told you, you could check that my guns have never been fired. Both the Colt an' the Winchester have had a taste of creek water, though. I'll go an' get the shoulder gun, if you like.'

Burrows slumped into his swivel chair, and Bob went out to get the Winchester. The marshal maintained a poker expression until he had examined both weapons, but when he had finished he pronounced himself satisfied that neither of them had been fired.

'Well, Bob, I must admit I had you figured for a killer when you hitched up outside this office, but I don't hold that view no more, now. Maybe you ought to pay a visit to the sheriff's office an' tell him what you told me about the way Curly met his end. What do you say?'

Bob grinned and stood up. 'Is Wilbur Strong still in office as county sheriff?'

'He sure is, but he may be out of

town at this time. You might have to talk with his deputy. That would be Rex Patrick, I guess.'

'Okay, then, I'll contact the sheriff's office and the undertaker,' Bob agreed. 'Maybe we'll run into one another again in the near future.'

Burrows showed him out and then went back to his chair, where he slumped and tilted back his hat. His mind was full of the recent visit and the sudden death of Curly Thomas. He wondered who Thomas' enemies were, and what he had done to merit being shot to death when another man was seeking him over a trifling misdemeanour.

Burrows was assuming that Bob McCleave was thoroughly honest, and this far he had no special reason to think otherwise. The army bred gun handlers, but not cold-blooded killers. If the McCleaves were not involved in the killing, then there were probably more ruthless guns in and around the county seat than he, Burrows, knew about.

An hour after dusk, a series of unholy noises began to disturb the comparative peace of Main Street. The sounds of merriment were drowned at short intervals by voices raised in anger and the sickening thuds of bunched fists hitting flesh.

Marshal Burrows had done a few turns round the main night spots and his deputy was doing the leg work at the time when the altercations started. Slim came to his feet, but as he had just finished his supper, he was not keen to leave the office unattended to sort out the offender himself.

Five minutes slipped by while the town marshal paced the scarred boards of the floor and awaited new developments. When his patience had almost given out, a brief glance into the street showed that his deputy, Carlos Santos, a Texican, was coping, though with difficulty.

Santos, a dark burly man with bushy black hair and brows, was coming down the sidewalk in the direction of the office, supporting and restraining another active young man, namely, Jerry Lester, the artist. Lester had twice before knocked off Santos' flat, grey, curly-brimmed stetson with unexpected side swipes. Santos, although he did not like the punishment which was being meted out to him, was a patient man. He was loath to hit a man over the head with a gun butt unless it was absolutely necessary.

Two minutes later, deputy and arrested man arrived at the office door and almost fell through it. Burrows blocked their way with a sour expression on his face and his hands on his hips.

'So what in tarnation have we got here, Carlos? Ain't this fellow the painter, who's makin' a picture of the bank?'

Carlos started to nod rather painfully. He had been punched in the neck a couple of times, and he felt quite a bit under par.

'This is the painter, marshal. Name of Jerry Lester. Gave no trouble until tonight. Now he is goin' round the town accusin' a lot of men of havin' stolen his paintin'. Me, I didn't think it was any good to start with, but you know how these artists go on about their work!'

'What did he do exactly?'

Lester's handsome fresh-complexioned face was beaded with perspiration. His cream stetson was jammed well forward on his head after acquiring a thick sheen of street dirt from hard contact with the earth. His blue eyes, which were slightly glassy, focussed upon the marshal with some difficulty.

'What has he done, indeed?' Lester echoed. 'He's done nothin' more than try an' trace his work which was stolen off the easel while he was not lookin'. Doggone it, marshal, you peace officers ought to be helpin' in the search rather than pickin' a quarrel with the likes of me. I don't like the way your deputy is handlin' things at all!'

Lester's outburst left him breathless, and gave Santos a chance to report on his conduct. 'This far, he's broken a saloon window, an' had a fight with two townsmen. Apart from spillin' a lot of other men's drink an' upsettin' a table — '

'An' he's struck an officer out of *my* office, who was carryin' out his routine duties,' Burrows cut in heavily. 'That's enough for me. He spends this night at least in a cell. Maybe if he's lucky, the men he's assaulted an' wrongfully accused won't prefer charges against him.'

Lester tensed himself and filled his lungs for another loud outburst of protest, but suddenly Burrows was alongside him. Between them the two peace officers caught him off-balance and heaved him into the first of the two cells at the back of the office. Slim slammed the door, and Carlos worked the key in the lock.

They stood back as Lester let out a roar of anguish which threatened to grow louder. No sort of protests had any effect upon him, and it was not until the marshal resorted to shock tactics that the situation in the office improved. A fire bucket full of dirty water had the desired effect, eventually, and, as Lester slipped into a noisy fitful sleep, the peace officers managed to work up sufficient interest to discuss the puzzling theft of the artist's work.

4

As Slim Burrows had suggested, Sheriff Wilbur Strong was out of town on the day when Bob McCleave wanted to contact him. Rex Patrick, the sheriff's chief deputy, listened to what Bob had to say and promised to inform the sheriff as soon as he returned to town from Rockwall.

Rod Pike, the veteran undertaker, took charge of the shattered corpse of Curly Thomas, and that left Bob free to return to the Diamond M and converse further with his father. Arthur McCleave was as surprised as anyone else when he heard about the way in which the unfortunate trickster had met his end. But he had lived a long time, and as the boss of a thriving concern he was glad to wash his hands of the whole affair, knowing full well that no other ordinary hand would attempt to take off with

Diamond M money in future without first reflecting upon Thomas' death.

* * *

Two days later, the McCleaves had another consignment of freight on trail between Broad Creek and Rockwall, this time going in a northerly direction from the county seat. Bob was riding as unofficial escort to two wagons, but he was almost a quarter of a mile in the rear of the convoy. For upwards of two hours the wagons rolled towards the north, and it was when they were approaching the same ridge where the attack had developed earlier that Bob had his first touch of uneasiness.

Perhaps half a mile away to the west side of the trail he had caught a brief flash of reflected sunlight on high ground. Too far away, he thought, to be a party planning a raid in the vicinity of the ridge, but there might have been some sort of lookout party signalling to men hidden nearer.

Some ten minutes later, a view from the top of a small gradient confirmed that riders were rapidly approaching the wagons from the opposite direction. Bob tensed up and increased the speed of his mount, fully expecting that the wagons would be attacked and that he had positioned himself too far away to afford them any protection.

For once, however, his worst fears were not realized. The converging riders were Sheriff Strong and three temporary deputies, returning from Rockwall where they had been delayed on a special assignment.

The riding party had already halted beside the lead wagon when Bob arrived in a cloud of dust with his Winchester held across his chest. The small posse had tensed up on account of his mode of approach in spite of the warning given by Dan Rees that young McCleave was coming up fast.

Wilbur Strong was the first to relax. He laughed, quietly at first and then more gustily, when he saw that Bob had recognized them for what they were.

'Well if it ain't young Bob, fresh from the army and a polished cavalry saddle! It sure is good to see you again, Bob, an' to know you're as keen as you are to take care of your Pa's property! My, my, workin' for Uncle Sam sure has stiffened that backbone of yours.'

Strong was just turned fifty, a veteran in office with a Roman nose and a pointed chin, both good features which gave a clue to the way he carried out his duties. He brooked no nonsense from anyone. A barrel chest in a khaki shirt virtually hid a small paunch which had developed in the last ten years.

Even without the sheriff's star pinned to the white vest, Strong was an eye-catching figure. His brown eyes flashed under the brim of his undented dun stetson. He sat his big-barrelled stockingfoot roan as though he had been a cavalryman all his life.

'You didn't ever need stiffening in yours, Wilbur,' Bob returned warmly. 'By the way, did you see any signs of unwanted activity uptrail a piece?'

The sheriff's face hardened a little. 'Nothing at all worth mentioning, Bob. If you ask me, your timely appearance the other day scared off the wrongdoers. Now, why don't you turn around an' come back to town with me? I don't figure you'll do any good actin' as a rear guard to these two wagons.'

Bob was about to protest, but Rees was the first to speak. 'Them's my sentiments, master Bob. Go back with the sheriff an' tell him about the latest happenings while he's been out of town.'

Bob clearly wanted to talk privately with Sheriff Strong, but he still doubted whether he should allow the wagons to proceed north unattended. A concerted argument took place with Strong, Rees, Rees Junior and one of the deputies talking persuasively before Bob managed to get the better of his doubts and turn his mount's head towards the south.

Just before the riders and the wagons

parted, he called to the older Rees, 'If anyone looks like givin' you trouble discharge your heaviest weapon in the air, Dan! The sound will carry quite a long way!'

The veteran protested that he would do that in any case, and finally the riders came away in the direction of the county seat. Strong took the first opportunity which presented itself to have Bob tell him about recent developments since he had been away from his office. The story of Curly Thomas, his wrong-doings and his untimely end were recounted in full detail, together with the scant knowledge which Bob had concerning the killers and their possible movements.

Strong cleared his throat and rowelled his stockingfoot into giving a little more speed. Bob perceived his intention and did the same. They drew a little further ahead of the three deputies in order to talk without being overheard.

'Bob, I could use you as a deputy.

How about wearin' a star an' backin' me over the trails of this county for a while? You could be watchin' your father's freight at the same time, as well as doin' me a favour an' the county a lot of good. What do you say? Are you good an' ready to settle on the ranch with your accountant and blacksmith brothers-in law?'

Bob gave his brief wry smile and shook his head in answer to the latter query. 'Do you think I could work for you an' support Pa's interests at the same time?'

'With a little co-operation from me I'm sure you could, Bob, so why don't you give it a try?'

'Ask me when we get a little nearer town,' Bob requested, after a pause.

Strong did so, and when he asked again the answer was in the affirmative.

★　★　★

In the early hours of the afternoon, the centre of Broad Creek was at its quietest time of the day. Although it was a busy and prosperous town most of the business people managed to take an hour or so off for an unofficial siesta. This was widely known by businessmen who came in from other parts. For several years, the banks had been closing their doors during this period, and opening them again at three o'clock for further transactions.

Mr Van Duren, the manager of the South-Western National Bank, rested in his office. The three tellers went home, and returned punctually at three p.m. Bob McCleave, Sheriff Strong and the other returning riders were still some distance away from town on this important day when Leary Rice and Clint Richards, an older teller, headed towards the bank from the east end of town. Richards was in a poor state of health. He limped from an old war wound, as well as being almost stone deaf. His condition made Rice approach the building somewhat slower than he would have liked.

Rice could see young Terry Mackson, a youth of nineteen and the third teller, coming back to work from the other end of the street. He would have liked to get there ahead of Mackson and be in a position to warn him to start out earlier, but Richards' slowness prevented this.

As it was, Mackson, a short-sighted, rather pimply young man with a heavy fair quiff and a flabby face, just reached the locked door ahead of his seniors. Rice shrugged and sniffed, pushed him aside and applied his key to the lock.

At the back of the two hotels on the opposite side of the street a small group of men had gathered, along with their five horses. No one in authority had seen them approach, nor had anyone noted anything unusual about them. They knew what they were about, however, and after the briefest of conversations they left the horses to their minder, a black-eyed man with a goatee beard, and stepped down the alley beside the bigger of the two hotels in single file.

Anyone seeing them in other circumstances would have found it hard to remember anything they had in common. In fact they were bank robbers, and they shared the same rather precarious, risky profession, along with the love of the easy money it provided.

Striding along at their head was a very tall rangy individual in a complete black outfit. All black, except for a white square of cloth which he was taking from his pocket to use as a mask. Behind him was a shorter, more rotund man with a pockmarked face and an uneasy way of walking which suggested that he had a painful wound at belt level under his gaudy check shirt. He was toying with a red bandanna at his neck.

Third in line was the shortest of the group; a stocky man with long arms and short legs. He had a nose long enough to show up well, even with a slack blue bandanna over it. The fourth man was a flashy dresser with lace at his cuffs and neck. As he crossed the street, he was folding in half a fine red square of cloth which had never graced his neck.

For a few seconds they stopped outside the door of the bank. At a nod from their tall leader they donned their masks and stepped through the door after him. The big counter was down the right hand side of the front office, giving the cashiers about one-third of the office space in which to do their work. The rest was for the customers, and all they had to share it with were two potted plants and a hat-stand.

The raiders moved with precision. The leader strode straight across to the door on the rear wall which gave access to the manager's office. He positioned himself beside it with his back to the wall and quickly drew both his .44 Colts. The man in the red mask headed for the counter closely followed by the flashy dresser with the red silk square draped across his face. Both had their revolvers to hand.

The short, stocky man stayed inside

the street door as though specially detailed off to keep a sharp watch on it. He, too, was hefting his hardwear.

At the time of the quiet invasion, Leary Rice had his head inside the doors of the big safe against the right hand wall behind the counter. Young Terry Mackson, short-sighted and spotty, was dusting off the counter with a piece of yellow cloth. Old Clint Richards, the limping veteran, was standing behind the counter solemnly polishing his spectacles, and taking notice of no one in particular.

The man in the white mask said: 'All right, now listen an' listen good. This is a hold-up. Two of my men are comin' in there to fill some bags with money from the safe. If you tellers know what's good for you, you won't interfere. These guns are not worn for ornament!'

Young Mackson gasped and slowly raised his hands. Richards hooked on his spectacles, not having heard the warning, and then raised his hands. Rice backed out of the safe, not quite sure whether he ought to obey orders or make an effort to thwart the raid. A tray of coins slipped from his nervous fingers and spilled to the ground with an almighty clatter.

The pockmarked man and the dude ducked through the gap in the counter and came up watchful. The first of the pair blinked at Rice and fired a warning shot into the door of the safe. It ricochetted off the metal and singed the cashier's coat along the shoulder. He flinched and raised his hands as high as they would go.

'Get a move on,' the leader suggested.

There was the sound of footsteps in the back room. The door was abruptly thrown open, and the manager, Mr Van Duren, a fifty-seven year old Dutch-American appeared in the opening holding a cigar like a dagger. He was a full-faced man whose black hair was rapidly thinning and showing a lot of grey on either side of the centre parting.

The small jumpy outlaw by the door reacted at once, firing three shots around the door space, all of which went within a few inches of the startled official. Van Duren jumped back into his office and slammed the door. Another bullet partially shattered a panel, but no attempt was made to go in after him.

The fancy dresser walked up behind Richards and Mackson and hit them one at a time behind the ear with one of his guns. They slumped to the ground and took no further interest in the proceedings. Rice, who could not stand physical pain, hopped around and kept his distance while the two collectors filled bags, closely watched by the other two.

'Take a look outside, Shorty,' the leader ordered, when the packing was almost completed.

The small man did as he was ordered. He came back a few seconds later. 'Jinx has the horses ready in the mouth of the alley opposite. There's men's heads showin' up an' down the street, but they ain't aimin' to come any closer. Are we ready to vamoose?'

'Sure, out you go, tell Jinx to turn the horses round. We're goin' out the same way as we came, see? We'll follow in a minute!'

Shorty always got nervous when he heard of last minute changes of plan. He had expected to gallop off down the main street: now they were going out through the vacant space behind the two hotels at the other side of the thoroughfare. He frowned at his leader, but the latter seemed just as calm as ever. Calmer, if anything.

Shorty moved out. He crossed the street, walking purposefully on his short legs, and gave the instruction to his partner, the horse minder. Jinx briefly rubbed a patch of scar tissue over his right eyebrow, and then he complied with the request. This was no time for an argument. The getaway on these occasions was always a critical time.

The men with the bags staggered into

view. A rifle bullet flew high over their heads, and men could be seen wondering if they dared blaze off a few shots at the raiders. The leader paused long enough to fire half a dozen bullets to dissuade the would-be heroes. He then ran the last few yards across the dirt of the street and leapt into the saddle of a black stallion.

This splendid animal forced its way through the other horses and headed down the alley, closely followed by the other four riders, none of whom were keen to be the last out of town.

As the clatter of hooves receded, men came out into the open brandishing weapons. Leary Rice came out of the bank, cautiously followed by Manager Van Duren. The first comers were slow to raise their voices.

5

Deputy Sheriff Rex Patrick was a quiet, thoughtful individual with a luxuriant growth of brown hair. He was the only man in town whose neatly trimmed moustache grew into his tapering sideburns. He was thirty years of age. Many women with marriageable daughters talked politely to him every time their paths crossed. The men found him civil enough, but some wondered if he might not be found wanting in the sort of emergency which cropped up every now and again for peace officers.

By twenty after three on the day of the raid, the whole town of Broad Creek was in uproar. Town Marshal Burrows, and his deputy, Santos, had left their office in a hurry and interviewed the bank manager almost before he had recovered his breath.

Perspiration was starting from Burrows'

brow when he turned to his man and ordered him to go and ring the bell which hung in the town square. Santos knew that the ringing of the bell was the signal to summon a posse. He wondered what Burrows really had in mind, but after the briefest of pauses he hurried away to carry out the instructions.

The ears of the townsfolk had been ringing to the sounds of the bell for all of two minutes when Deputy Patrick came up the sidewalk towards the bank looking very preoccupied. He had hoped to duck the business of personally raising a posse in the sheriff's absence, but now the damage was done. Someone had called the riders. For a minute or more his temper flared. He pushed his way through the thick group of angry men to the side of the town marshal, who surveyed him with raised brows.

'Marshal, do you have any idea who rang the bell?'

Slim blinked at him and flared his nostrils. 'Sure, Rex, it was Carlos, my deputy. I sent him along there to ring it. We're doin' you a favour. The bank's been robbed if you ain't heard. It's your business to round up a posse. The raiders all doubled about an' went west. Almost everyone in town heard their horses cross the bridge!'

Patrick's skin was white under the tan. He was trying to contain his anger. Burrows watched him. So did the bank manager, and presently Santos was back and beside them.

'The volunteers are musterin' outside your office, Mr Deputy,' Santos remarked quietly.

Patrick rumbled inwardly. He thumped a supporting post with his fist and finally took himself off to gather up the necessary riders. Some of the more mature townsmen stared after him, clicking their tongues and shaking their heads. Patrick was all right when Wilbur Strong was around: without the sheriff he was a nobody.

★　★　★

The echoing sounds of the town bell drew Bob McCleave and the sheriff's party in with all the speed they could muster on tired horses.

Strong rode right up to the bank and listened patiently while Van Duren told him all over again what had happened. Bob also fumed. He, it was, who sent a message to the big livery which worked in conjunction with Diamond M freighters. Some five minutes elapsed, during which two livery hands came along with five spare horses. These latter could not match the tired ones for stamina, but at least they were fresh.

Strong, his three deputies and Bob exchanged horses without comment. No one seemed surprised when they had at once elected to go after the raiders as a second posse. Others saw to the cinching while they took a short drink and mopped themselves down. Bob was the first to mount up on his fresh horse. Strong lined up beside him and they cantered off down the street with the trio close behind them.

'Over the bridge, or not, Wilbur?' Bob queried crisply.

'We stay this side,' the sheriff replied.

He glanced at Bob's face to know his reaction and noted a smile spreading over the latter's tanned, serious face. Bob was thinking that not many hours had elapsed since he came this way before, looking for Curly Thomas. The smile faded as he reflected that the runaway bank robbers were likely to prove far more elusive than Thomas had done.

Strong set up a good pace. As they rode they kept watch on the winding creek in order to make sure that no one was hiding across from them, or seeking to double back unseen. Soon the spot where Bob had crossed under fire had gone by. The ground grew more rocky. It was more difficult to stay close to the waterway.

Within another mile it was hidden from them by rocks and foliage. And still the sheriff pressed on. Presently, Bob McCleave's aged claybank's neck began to droop. Its breathing became laboured, and finally a third small setback made Bob think that he was not going to be much good to his new master this trip. A plate began to work loose on one of the claybank's fore hooves.

Strong glanced back. 'What gives, amigo?' he called breathlessly.

'Bellows to mend, and now a shoe workin' loose, Wilbur. I sure am sorry about this.'

'Don't fret yourself none, amigo, it could happen to anybody. If you drop behind, keep a sharp lookout. There's always a chance you might turn up a renegade hidin' out after horse trouble same as you're havin' yourself.'

'I'll remember that, sheriff,' Bob called again. He hauled the claybank to one side and gave rather a peremptory wave to the trio who followed him. One man looked as if he was considering a change of horse with the disappointed young man, but somehow the offer was never made.

Bob dropped slowly further and further behind and finally swung out of the saddle when an upgrade began to overtax the struggling horse. He slackened the cinch strap and squatted on a rock while the limping animal recovered its breath and went in search of bunch grass to its liking.

Bob rolled a smoke and sucked contentedly on it for a minute or more. Strong and the other three were well above him by then, heading towards a break in the landscape between an outcrop of granite and a scattering of waist high boulders. Tiredness this far had prevented Bob from collecting his Winchester and spyglass from the claybank which had strayed some fifty yards from him.

Now, he felt the need to watch the progress of his labouring partners on the high ground. He scrambled off his rock and plodded up-trail after the claybank, but a sudden burst of firing distracted him, and left him standing like a petrified man with his eyes on the distant outcrop.

Rifle muzzles had briefly belched flame up there, and a toll of sorts had been taken of the peace officers' quartette. None of the four could be seen any longer. The rifles of the ambushers had either eliminated them or sent them to earth.

★ ★ ★

Sheriff Strong was a seething mass of hatred to all renegades as he ducked his head behind a protecting rock and thought over the recent happening which had almost sent him and his fellow riders prematurely to Boot Hill.

A sixth sense had warned him of impending trouble, but he had scarcely managed to utter a cry of warning when the first of the rifles firing from cover began to spew bullets at them. Strong, himself, had lived by a miracle. Two bullets had found a way through the upper half of his undented stetson without removing it. Only perspiration had kept it in place. In addition to that he had collected a faint shoulder burn and a rather painful knee.

One of his men had died with a bullet through his head, and another had sustained a wound in a fleshy part of his leg. The third was out of sight among rocks, but ominously silent when anyone called to him.

The bullets continued to fly for upwards of three minutes, during which time the peace officer was content to keep out of sight and stay intact. He and his men were in no shape to take up the pursuit, as one horse had galloped ahead of them; two more had ridden into a small cleared park between rocks, and would not be coaxed out while there was any sort of gunfire in the vicinity. The fourth had thrown up its fore feet, spilled its rider and gone back down the hill.

Strong and his party could have been eliminated in a very short time, except that the ambushers wanted to be miles away from the outcrop before the earlier posse — which they had eluded

— returned and took them in the rear.

The faint sounds of a withdrawal could be heard, but such a position as the sheriff was in did not call for a counter-attack against long odds. Strong ground his teeth, but refrained from giving any orders to his men. Five quiet minutes elapsed before he stood up and tried his painful knee. He was able to put his weight upon it, although he had to limp.

Barney Heap, the silent rider, was found to be suffering from prolonged unconsciousness due to a blow on the head when he threw himself into the rocks. A drink of water helped to revive him. Next, the man with the leg wound was given attention. Strong, himself, found and recovered the two horses in the park. By that time, he was ready to retrace his tracks.

Heap, with a wet bandanna clapped to his head, led one horse, while Strong moved at the head of the other which had the wounded man on its back. Need-less to say, the dead man was jack-knifed across the back of the first horse.

Fifteen minutes elapsed before the plodding men and horses got back to the spot where Bob McCleave had dismounted.

Bob had spent a few minutes trying to fix the loose horseshoe, but his efforts had been unsuccessful. He rose from behind a rock, feeling rather self-conscious as Strong and the others came abreast of him.

'Sorry I wasn't up there to give you a hand out when you needed me,' he began, apologetically.

'Think nothing of it, son,' Strong returned, 'you might have been dead, same as poor Cy Willis. They jumped us jest when we were at the top, an' they couldn't have picked a better spot or time to do the job, either. It wouldn't surprise me if one of them jaspers had Indian blood in him. First, they give Rex Patrick an' the other posse the slip, then they jump us so easy it might have been our first time out on a jaunt like this.'

Bob murmured words of commiseration. He led the claybank forward and insisted that the sheriff should ride it, at least for a while. Reluctantly, Strong agreed. As his body hit the saddle, he hunched and showed his fatigue fully for the first time.

As the downcast little outfit slowly backtracked towards town, Bob's face, which had been thoughtful, brightened. In his hand he was swinging what looked like a black cylinder or tube, made out of some light material.

About half an hour later, Strong, who had been dozing fitfully, willed himself wide awake, and noticed the object clearly for the first time. His curiosity became stronger than his fatigue.

'Bob, what in tarnation is that you're danglin' in your hand? Don't tell me it is some sort of secret weapon doled out by the US cavalry for special occasions?'

Bob chuckled. His spirits had risen, even though they had a dead man in their midst. 'If I asked you to guess what it was, Wilbur, I don't figure you could name it. So I'll give you a clue.

It's a roll of canvas. I found it on the ground jest before I relieved this crowbait claybank of my Winchester an' spyglass. Know what it's for?'

'I don't have the vaguest idea, amigo. Supposin' you tell me all about it.'

'It's a paintin', Wilbur. An' not jest any old paintin' either! Maybe you saw that young artist fellow around town. The one who was doin' a paintin' of the bank! Well, this is it! The paintin' of the bank itself! The one the artist claimed was stolen!'

Bob relinquished his hold on the reins, stepped a yard to one side and unrolled the painting with something of a flourish. Strong, Heap and the wounded man all glanced across at it, but their interest was short-lived. The sheriff, perhaps, summed up the feelings of them all.

He groaned. 'The bank is robbed. My riders are jumped. I'm grooved. My stomach thinks my throat is cut. My water canteen is empty, an' my new boy shows me a paintin' of a bank an'

79

expects me to enthuse over it. Aw, have a heart, Bob. Now, if that had been a gatlin' gun an' you'd been up the hill with us a while back, in time to use it on the robbers, I could have applauded. But not at that paintin'. Why don't you lose it, toss it back on the ground where you found it, huh?'

Bob was annoyed, but he did not show it. Instead, he rolled up the canvas and stuffed it through his belt. Without more ado, he grabbed the reins and encouraged the claybank to a slightly faster pace.

6

The discomfited quintette created quite a stir when they trudged back into town with the sad tale of their reversal written on their faces. Three of them needed the services of the doctor; one was ready for planting and Bob, the fifth man, wanted to crawl away somewhere and try to forget the outcome of his first active ride as an assistant to the sheriff.

Promising to get in touch, he left at the earliest possible moment and made his way to a hotel, the Creekwater, where he booked himself a room and asked for a bath. Jerry Lester's painting of the bank was jettisoned upon the floor while Bob rested his tired body in the bath tub.

For a time, he was almost asleep in the water. When he began to rouse himself, however, the painting caught his eye again. He knew what it looked like without unfurling it. He also knew sufficient to know that the artist had real talent. Painting a bank building, though, was a rather unusual choice of subject. He wondered if Lester had painted it with the idea of selling his effort, or if he had done it just to please himself. Not many people could afford to paint just to indulge their own fancies, and Lester did not look the type of fellow to have any sort of private income.

The painter's spell in the cell had been a short one. Burrows had let him out at breakfast time the following morning and warned him to keep out of trouble, even though losing a painting might be deemed to be provocation of sorts in some parts. Lester had reiterated his protest and gone on his way.

Now, the painting had been found, but where was Lester? The more Bob thought about it, the less keen he was to rush out and find the artist. Wilbur

Strong had seemed anything but keen to better his association with Bob when they had parted, but he would certainly not object to a little quiet investigating into the painting and how it was executed.

One new line of thought kept the ex-cavalryman from feeling depressed. Either the artist had found his painting and dropped it on the way out of town, heading eastward, or, whoever had earlier misappropriated it had dropped it along the same route.

The route was an unusual one. It was not beyond the bounds of possibility that the raiders themselves had grabbed the painting and since lost it. Bob wondered, and smiled. Soon, his spirits were rising again, and he was happy to be out of the bath and drying himself.

He brushed the dust out of his trail-riding outfit, donned a clean shirt and dressed himself to go out of doors. Almost as an afterthought, he picked up the painting and took it with him.

In the nearest bar, he found himself a

stool and waited for the barman's attention.

'A beer for me, an' one for yourself,' he murmured, leaning forward in a conspiratorial fashion.

The face of the fleshy barman brightened at the mention of a free beer. He came back to deliver two foaming mugs, and found the piece of canvas half-unrolled on the bar top. His moustache spread like that of a walrus as he applied the mug to his lips. Only then would he condescend to show any interest in the painting, which Bob was holding out to him.

On one side there was a Quaker shopkeeper, drinking a non-alcoholic drink. The other way were two farmers whose clothing showed their prosperity. It was the farmers who showed mild interest in the unrolling of the canvas. The barman took his cue from them.

'Yer, a nice paintin' mister, but not the sort of thing I'd like for myself. Everybody knows it's the South-Western National Bank. It don't seem right to me, showin' a picture of the bank when it's jest been robbed. Thanks for the beer.'

The barman moved away pointedly. So did the farmers. And that seemed to be the general attitude of a few other men who glimpsed the painting. They acted as if the showing of it was in bad taste.

Bob's stomach was rumbling with emptiness, but he put off food for a while longer, in an effort to get the opinion of others about the painting. A long-established liveryman eyed it over and soon lost interest. He recognized it for what it was, and had no questions to ask about where it had been found, or where the artist had gone.

The young man tried the reaction of a saddler who had known his father for a long time, and this old practitioner, a man of few words, had one comment to make: 'A man who would hang about for hours paintin' a picture of the outside of a bank has to be a no good.'

The next stopping place was the

eating house of an Englishman named Matthews. Joe Matthews was in his middle fifties, a former seaman who had come ashore in San Francisco for the last time, and finally settled in Broad Creek.

Bob met Joe with the width of the serving counter between them. Matthews frowned and gave his brown moustache a gentle touch at the ends.

'You've had a busy day by all accounts, Bob,' he murmured. 'You must be hungry, but I'm hoping you aren't going to offer that painting to pay for the food!'

The Englishman's lined face was eased by a grin.

'Have you seen it before?' Bob asked.

'Of course. Hasn't every man in town taken a free look at it? That is, until somebody got tired of seein' it and removed it for a joke. What will you have to eat?'

'Beef and vegetables. Fruit pie. And coffee to start off with, if you have some on the boil.'

Joe nodded and promised quick service on all counts. The long narrow cafe was steamy. Still seeking publicity for his actions, Bob rested the canvas across the top of a hat stand. Twice while he was eating his food, men went by and knocked it down. They picked it up on each occasion, noted what it was, and replaced it rather solemnly, after noting whose possession it was in.

No one had expressed any special curiosity about Jerry Lester. In a place like Broad Creek, however, there would be talk. And sooner or later the talk would get back to the painter, if he was still interested and was still in town.

Jerry Lester, when he went drinking, was a loner, a man who drank by himself and one who never sought the company of another drinker while the prolonged quenching of the thirst was taking place. In bars, he was a man of little conversation: nevertheless, he liked to hear the content of other's men's discussions.

His hearing was particularly good.

He heard mention of the recovery of his painting on three occasions when the men who were talking about it had deliberately lowered their voices.

By this particular time, his interest in the bank painting had waned. He had other interest, and yet it was difficult to remain totally indifferent to a piece of his work. Especially one for which he had already spent a night in a cell.

Jerry had a long-term chip on his shoulders. His eavesdropping suggested that many hours had elapsed since the finder of his canvas had returned to town. It should have been returned to him, or at least handed in to the peace office for return by the town marshal. This young ex-soldier was hanging onto it for some reason or another. A few direct questions could have led to the recovery of his — Lester's — new piece of work. But young McCleave did not seem to have bothered about that.

Perhaps he expected a visit from the owner of the canvas? The more Jerry thought about it, the more he felt that

McCleave wanted him to make contact. But why was he so interested? Could he have an inkling of the truth about the painting?

Jerry emptied his glass again, refused a refill and sauntered out into the open air, propping his body against a post which held up the sidewalk awning. McCleave had ridden with the sheriff, but now he was resting up in a room at the Creekwater. The hotel of that name was about one hundred yards off, down the street.

Jerry fished in his shirt pocket and brought out a small cigar, which he stuck in his mouth. The match to light it took a little longer to find, but he discovered it eventually and rasped it on his thumb nail.

While he was still sucking on the fragrant weed a new idea came to him. It made him smile. He decided that he would give McCleave a chance to say where he found the elusive canvas, and then pretend that he did not believe him.

Such an attitude would lead to trouble, of course, but Jerry was not troubled by that consideration. After all, many of his recent business dealings had left him angry. It would do him good to lash out at somebody for a change. The cigar was cocked at a jaunty angle in his mouth as he strode off towards the Creekwater hotel.

* * *

The knock on Bob's door was a light one, but the sleeper roused himself immediately. It did not occur to him that the knock might mean that someone had knocked on the wrong door, or was somehow in error.

He called out: 'Jest hold on a minute, I won't keep you long.'

He slid out of bed and catfooted around the end of it where his pants were hanging over an upright chair. His back was towards the door as he slid first one leg and then the other into the trousers. A slight draught of air caused him to turn round before he had adjusted his belt, and in so doing he discovered to his surprise that the door was wide open, and that a man's bulk was framed in the opening.

His first reaction was one of anger. This was Jerry Lester, the painter, with a cigar stuck in the corner of his mouth. The expression on the newcomer's face was scarcely a friendly one. He was wide awake, and as like as not primed with liquor. Moccasins went a little way towards explaining the quietness of his entry.

Bob finished tightening his belt. He wagged a finger at Lester.

'Now see here, mister, I asked you to wait a while. Jest because I answered your knock that don't give you the right to burst right in here! Me, I'm not used to havin' strangers barge into my room when the door is closed for the night!'

Bob was shifting his weight from one bare foot to the other. Lester had moved in a yard or so, but he was crouched and gave no sign whether he was coming further into the room, or not. The painter stabbed a finger at Bob's chest. When he had made his gesture, he pointed the finger at the hanging lamp in the centre of the room.

'How about lightin' the lamp, amigo? Then we can close the door. The air tends to get cool after nightfall.'

Bob, who was seething with anger, even though he had half-expected a visit from this man, hesitated and then moved towards the lamp in question. He lit it and then backed off, not quite sure how the interview was going to go.

At length he placed his hands on his hips. 'It had to be something urgent, something important to you,' he began.

Lester rolled the cigar around his lips. He did it rather expertly, as though he had grown up with such expensive smokes for comfort.

'You have an item of my property. You've been goin' round the town, tellin' people about it. What you should have been doin' was findin' out where I was. The paintin' was stolen, an' you ought to be seein' about its return.'

Bob's eyes slipped away to the chest of drawers, an article of furniture which was against a wall, and almost equidistant from either of them. The rolled canvas lay on top of the chest, along with various small items out of Bob's pockets. Lester noted where it was.

'How come you didn't hand it into the marshal's office, amigo?'

For the first time the ghost of a smile flitted across Bob's face. 'In case you didn't know it, the peace officers of this town an' county have been kind of busy in this last day or two. They had other, more important things on their minds.'

'You couldn't have found out where I was, could you?'

Bob shrugged, 'I figured you weren't any longer interested in it. Maybe you'd left town. I didn't know.'

Moving with surprising ease, Lester crossed to the chest and unfurled the painting. It had suffered a little through being thrust through Bob's belt, but the damage was slight.

'Where did you say you found it, McCleave?'

'I didn't, but I can tell you it was dropped by someone usin' a certain route out of town. Towards the east, north of the lesser creek. In fact right on the route taken by the bank robbers directly they'd left town.'

'Do you mean that?' Lester queried, as he rolled up the canvas.

Bob nodded. Lester appeared to grow angry.

'What you are sayin' is that I'm tied in with the bank robbers withdrawal. Is that it?'

Greatly relaxed, Bob replied: 'You can put any interpretation upon my words which suits you, mister. All I stated was the facts. Where did you drop it?'

Lester tensed. 'You know I went into cells for tryin' to locate it after it was stolen! Now you're makin' out I lost it, that it wasn't stolen at all! I wonder if you have any idea how an artist feels when his work is stolen?'

Bob shrugged his shoulders. He had half-turned towards the window, toying with the idea of opening it wider, when Lester's fist connected with his cheekbone and sent him down in a heap beside the chest of drawers.

The butt of the cigar was withdrawn and placed on the furniture, along with the painting. Rubbing his cheek rather gingerly, Bob slowly rose to his feet.

'Say, Lester, you ain't as drunk as you like to make out you are!'

Bob put up his hands, but his opponent came forward quickly and swung again, twice. In avoiding the second punch, the darker man's tousled hair brushed the underside of the hanging lamp, causing the moving shadows to alter shape and affect the fight.

The fighters stayed closer after that, trading punches. They were both tall, and only a few pounds in weight separated them. A punch which landed high sent Lester's cream stetson spinning off his head. The painter partially rode the punch, however, and retaliated in a way most unexpected.

Largely due to the swinging of the lamp, Lester was able to advance a moccasined foot unobserved. He feinted with a punch, and, instead, dropped his leather-shod foot upon one of his opponent's bare ones. Bob tried to pull back and failed. He was still off-balance when a body blow winded him. A swing to the head landed, and he was thrown sideways, to fall heavily against the drawers.

A wooden handle connected with his temple. His senses reeled. He slid to the floor with a sinking sensation in his stomach. For a few seconds, Lester bent over him with a slightly anxious expression on his face.

Presently, the victor straightened up. He extinguished the lamp, collected his painting and his cigar and left the room, closing the door behind him.

7

Within five minutes Bob had recovered sufficiently to scramble to his feet and stretch out on the bed. His head cleared rather slowly, and a throbbing went on in a blood vessel behind his temple for more than half an hour.

As soon as he felt steadier, he crossed to the window and gradually restored a feeling of well-being by breathing in deep gulps of fresh air. Lester had out-smarted him with a trick. Not that it mattered an awful lot. He had a feeling the fellow was staying in town. They would meet again. The most interesting part of the encounter was the painter's reaction to Bob's suggestion that he had lost the painting up-country from the lesser creek.

But for an occasional shooting pain in the head, he would have liked to have thought over all the possibilities connected with the painting in great detail. As it was, he bathed his head with a water pitcher's contents, drank a half pint of the same liquid and settled himself back to sleep.

★   ★   ★

The sun was illuminating the dust motes in the room when the sleeper awoke again. His temple was still rather painful, and he was not in any hurry to walk around. He thought about getting up for a while, without enthusiasm. The distant sound of walking horses finally prompted him to dress. He felt sure that Rex Patrick and the first posse were just returning to town.

★   ★   ★

The posse scattered quietly. Rex Patrick, hunched like the rest, with fatigue, tied his cayuse outside the sheriff's office and slouched indoors. As he crossed the floor, Strong, who was sleeping on a

98

camp bed, blinked his eyes and raised his head upon an elbow.

'Howdy, Rex. How did the riders give you the slip?'

Patrick was thinking that his superior might have given him a minute or two in which to rest up before starting his interrogation, but he had worked with Wilbur Strong for too long to delay giving information on occasions like this.

'They had us follow one or two spare horses, while they ducked out an' hid by the side of the creek. After we'd gone on, they crossed over I guess. But we didn't find out for a while. Then we started to backtrack, an' look for sign. Some of the boys couldn't agree as to where they'd crossed over. We lost time.

'Later, we found they'd crossed a whole lot earlier than we gave 'em credit for. We heard gunfire back there, an' we guessed you'd been out ridin' after them. Or they'd accidentally bumped into some other law abidin' group.'

Patrick propped himself up on the end of the desk and looked to Strong for clarification.

'They were firin' on me an' the boys, fresh from Rockwall, only we weren't fresh at all. An' they didn't do us one little bit of good, either. A friend of yours, Cy Willis, ducked into a bullet with his head. Died instantly. Another fellow was wounded, an' Bob McCleave's mount gave out on him.

'When you finally crossed the lesser creek, did you pick up any sign, anything to show which way they travelled after they'd jumped us from behind that outcrop?'

'Quite a time had elapsed by the time we got there, sheriff. The boys an' me, we reckoned they'd headed north. But the light faded while we were still lookin' for sign. So we didn't make much progress. After that, they could have gone either east or west. I couldn't say for sure.'

'Or north again, or down a big hole into the bowels of the earth,' Strong added miserably. 'All right, go home an' get your boots off. The rest of the details will do later.'

Patrick sighed as he was dismissed, but he hovered in the doorway as though he had a question to ask. Strong flung aside his blanket, came to his feet with an effort and went in search of the coffee pot.

'What other problem do you have, Rex?' he asked, talking over his shoulder.

'Did you say Bob McCleave was with you on the ride east?'

'I did, an' he's joining this office, if he ain't thought better of it in the night. So if you see him, make out he's welcome to work on this staff. Understand?'

Patrick nodded rather dumbly. He felt that the acquisition of Bob McCleave meant that he himself was in some way not up to his job as the sheriff's chief deputy. He left the building, and avoided Bob, who was coming down the street, using the sidewalk on the opposite side.

Ten minutes was long enough for Bob to accept the deputy's badge from Wilbur Strong and to ask permission to look a little further into the matter of the painting of the bank, and the man who had thought fit to paint it. Strong was feeling liverish and out of sorts with himself. He was in no mood to discuss theories with his new man, although he was pleased that Bob had gone along to see him at a reasonable hour.

Bob, in spite of his beating of the previous evening, was in good spirits. He felt sure that he could give a better account of himself if he encountered Jerry Lester in the bright light of day. He wanted his breakfast, and at the same time he favoured a little exercise prior to the meal.

Without knowing quite why, he found his footsteps heading up Second Street. Up ahead of him, he spied a familiar figure dragging a wooden packing case out of an office. Wilson

Hargrove was stripped of his grey frockcoat. His derby was jammed down hard on the back of his head. His teeth were mauling the last inch and a half of a cigar.

Hargrove grew tired of hauling the case. He dumped it on the sidewalk, straightened up and took a look up and down the street. His brows went up when he saw Bob, but his expression softened, and he called out while they were still separated by several yards.

'Well, if it ain't young Mr McCleave! Say, if you're comin' along here with the idea of insurin' your Pa's goods now, you've left it too late. I'm packin' and jest about ready to move!'

Bob waved his hand. He chuckled, but waited until he was up with the other man before answering him. 'Shucks, I wasn't thinkin' of insurin', Mr Hargrove, but I'm mighty surprised to find you leavin' town. Was it so hard, then, to persuade the folks of Broad Creek to avail themselves of your services?'

Hargrove, who had a white protective apron stretched across his trousers and vest, nodded heavily. 'Much harder than I expected. Maybe that strike against your Pa's wagons made them all shy of an insurer. It's hard to say. All I know is that I got the feelin' a day ago that I ought to be movin' on. Pastures new, as the poets say, huh?'

Bob gave him a hand to drag the box of rubbish off the sidewalk and round into the alley.

'You goin' any place special, Mr Hargrove?'

'Right now, I couldn't answer that, Bob. I won't know if it's special until I know what sort of a reception I'm goin' to get. There's a whole lot of waitin' in my kind of business. It wouldn't do for a young man. He'd be too impatient.'

The pair chatted about this and that without being particularly informative for another five minutes before shaking hands and parting. Bob then made his way by another route back into Main Street, where the tantalizing smell of food drew him towards the eating houses. He could smell ham and eggs long before he reached the Englishman's place, and, for a change, he entered the establishment of a taciturn Pole.

The food was good, but the customers were few. As soon as Bob was satiated, he came out boldly with his question.

'Mr Polcek, do you have any idea where I could find that young painter who painted a picture of the bank?'

For a few seconds, the proprietor's expression remained as blank as that of an Indian, and then he smiled. 'There are other things a young man might want to paint. My advice to you is to try the high ground. Did you want another cup of coffee?'

Bob shook his head, paid up and thanked his informant profusely. He left the building with his brow furrowed in thought. There were only two small hills within the vicinity of Broad Creek. On one was the cemetery, Boot Hill, and on the other were one or two rather luxurious residences which belonged to wealthy people who had come out west to settle. Probably Jerry Lester had gone to earth in one of the detached houses on the second hill.

As soon as he was sure that he was on the right track, Bob borrowed a useful spyglass from a clockmaker known to his father. He set off on foot for the small district on the second hill. Some three hundred yards from it, he made himself as inconspicuous as possible under a spreading oak tree, and put the glass to his eye.

The two-storey wooden board house which he first surveyed showed him as much as he wanted to see. It was the residence of Mr Hubert Devere, a prosperous buyer and seller of mining claims. Devere, himself, a big ruddy, white-moustached man in his early sixties, was nowhere to be seen, but the apple of his eye, blonde Miss Dolores Devere, his daughter, was sprawled decorously in a swinging seat on the front gallery.

Lester was a little to one side, and off the verandah, wiih his easel, canvas and paints, but for some little time Bob's attention was fixed on the girl. Dolores was most probably the number one heiress in the county, yet few dared to think of courting her. Father had very definite ideas about sons-in-law, and he had enough influence to make life difficult for any young suitor who stayed around the place after he had disapproved.

Dolores was a beauty by any standards. She had a fresh complexion, Cupid's bow lips and heaped blonde wavy hair. For the painting she was decked out in an expensive pink dress with puffy short sleeves, and a low eye-catching neckline. Even as Bob studied her, Lester made some witty remark which sent the young woman into delightfully musical peals of laughter. Bob began to think that there was more to the painting business than he had at first thought.

The seat swung under the subject, creating a tiny breeze. From time to time, Dolores' mother, who was doing some sort of delicate needle work on the upper gallery, leaned out to see how her angelic daughter was getting on. The older woman seemed quite satisfied with the situation, although to Bob it seemed that Lester stared at his subject far more than was necessary.

The glass brought the canvas up close enough to make it clear that the artist really was painting the girl. The likeness was apparent, even through the lenses. It was obvious that the painting was not finished, so Lester was unlikely to leave town in a hurry, especially with such a charming subject.

Reluctantly, Bob telescoped his glass and prepared to return to the centre of town. He had other questions to ask, and he was anxious to get them asked before Wilbur Strong devised any sort of scheme for sending him out of town.

As he retraced his steps he toyed with his deputy's badge, which so far had remained hidden in his pocket. He wanted to ask questions at the bank. Maybe Mr Van Duren would give him a better reception if he was wearing the star.

8

Bob was conscious of the brightness of his new badge all the way down Main. Several people who did not know he had joined the sheriff's office called out to him and expressed their surprise and pleasure in finding he had become one of the town's peace officers.

On the threshold of the bank, the young man hesitated. He had not been inside the building since the raid had taken place. He wondered what sort of a reception he would receive from the bank employees. Two customers were at the counter when he went in. He hovered in the background, listening to the small talk and imagining the positioning of the bandits from the few details he had already heard.

One glance was sufficient to show that all three cashiers were back at work. Leary Rice was looking pale and peaked, but otherwise he was fit. Richards and Mackson both had bandaged heads, but the older man looked the worse for wear because his spectacles would not sit easily over the padding.

The first of the two customers left. Rice moved to deal with the business of the second one. Mackson glanced short-sightedly at Bob; he avoided contact and made a show of being occupied with his cash drawer. Richards bent over his ledger, examining his pen in the light of a lamp.

It was obvious by Rice's expression that Bob was not going to receive any special sort of welcome. If anything, as a junior peace officer he was due to be dismissed rather brusquely. A wealthy rancher's son had to be handled carefully, but a new badge wearer had to learn his place, especially in the premises of a big and prosperous bank.

Bob felt that he could just about read the chief cashier's thoughts. He was wondering about the possibility of a private interview with the branch manager when his eyes took in the spots on the rear wall where the bullets had landed. He could well imagine the speed with which Van Duren had withdrawn when the raider started to blast off at him.

From the bullet holes, Bob's attention wandered higher up the wall. Midway between the height of the door and the ceiling was a light rectangular patch with a nail above it, suggesting that a picture had hung there. He was still staring at the lighter coloured patch when Van Duren's door opened and the manager himself appeared in the opening.

Bob noted the brief look of apprehension: as if the manager experienced a renewal of the fear felt when he disturbed the raiders. Rice had just disposed of the second customer and was calling out to him, but Van Duren was a much better man to converse with, if he was in the mood.

The Dutchman blinked as he noticed

where Bob's attention was focussed. He, too, glanced up at the wall and saw the different coloured space where the picture had hung. Rice was coughing, clearing his throat purposefully, to no avail.

'Mr Rice, did you have any reason to move the picture from this wall?'

Rice and Mackson glanced up at the blank space. Seconds later, Richards noticed the situation and he took a look, also. All three tellers appeared to be completely mystified.

Rice replied: 'Why, er, no, Mr Van Duren, I, er, I didn't know the picture was missin' until my attention was drawn to it this very minute.'

'Really, my man, I don't know how you can work in this office all day and fail to notice a sudden change like that. I suppose you other two don't know anything about it, either?'

Mackson spoke up and answered in the negative. Richards was content to shake his head. Van Duren clicked his tongue as Bob moved closer to him, and presently the manager screwed a smile into his flabby face and beckoned him into the private office.

Bob entered and took off his hat. He walked around to the client's chair through sheer force of habit, but Van Duren gestured for him to use it when he hesitated. The manager flopped rather than sat in his own chair. He glanced rather pointedly at the deputy's badge and nodded his approval.

'Any news of the bank's funds, Mr Bob?'

'Sorry, nothing new this far, Mr Van Duren. So far as we know, the raiders got clear away, somewhere north of the lesser creek. But the trail may not be altogether dead. Why don't you tell me about that missin' picture out in the front office?'

Van Duren massaged a flabby cheek with the ball of his thumb. 'You don't think there could be a connection between the robbery an' the picture, do you?'

Bob grinned. 'How can I tell if you

don't explain to me? I'd like to know more about when it disappeared, if anyone can be precise about it. I heard tell that things above normal eye level tend to get overlooked, but I would have thought a big picture missin' from a front office around the time of a big robbery would have been noticed by someone.'

Bob sat further back, willing to give the manager plenty of time to explain. The restlessness of the older man's eyes betrayed the great amount of activity in his brain. He was trying to work out for himself the solution to the puzzle before he enlightened his visitor. Eventually, a light cough from Bob loosened his tongue.

'I'm sorry to keep you waiting, Bob. The picture was a painting of the founder of this chain of banks. As you know, we are now the South-Western National Bank, but it wasn't always so. The founder was a man named Jonathan Beauclerc. He did at one time reside in a place called Pecosville, further south in this territory.'

'Does Mr Beauclerc still have his money in the banks? Is he active?'

'I believe not,' Van Duren murmured. 'For some reason or another Mr Beauclerc had to sell out to another person, a man named Sinclair Hayton. The founder had a run of bad luck, so I was told. Anyway, it was his picture that graced the wall.'

Bob had a hazy recollection of the appearance of the man in the picture, but he asked for a description in words, which had Van Duren glancing at the ceiling and thinking hard.

'Let me see, Mr Beauclerc, yes. A man of about sixty-five years. Wore a wing collar. Had short, tufted brows and a somewhat lined face.'

Van Duren made lines on his own countenance between the sides of his nose and the outer ends of his mouth. 'Very steady eyes. Always wore a square cut black business suit. And that's about all I can tell you about him, which isn't bad seein' I've never laid eyes on the gentleman.' Van Duren hunched forward suddenly. 'Do you think the bank robbers took his picture?'

'I don't think it went at the time of the raid, otherwise Rice would have noticed. Either it went before, or after the raid.'

'But that would mean that an interloper entered this office at a time when the bank was closed,' Van Duren protested.

'It certainly looks that way,' Bob agreed.

'But if a man could get in undetected, why did they bother to come in through the front door with guns an' masks an' run a risk of bein' shot on the way out?'

'You have a very good question there, Mr Van Duren. One which certainly merits a deal of thought. But perhaps there was some difficulty over the keys. It might have been easier to get into the building than it was to break into the safe. You see what I mean?'

Van Duren nodded very decidedly. They talked for another five minutes, with the manager trying to plumb the depths of Bob's thoughts with only partial success. The older man seemed disappointed when his visitor left, and Rice looked eaten up with curiosity when Bob left by the front entrance, giving him only a curt nod.

Bob was thinking that if he could find the missing painting, he might trace the missing funds. Or, failing that, the painting might give an interesting clue to the whereabouts of the loot. He was whistling as he went up the street.

In the sheriff's office, he found Strong behind his desk, a pair of gold-rimmed spectacles low on his nose, apparently immersed in a heap of paper work. The sheriff looked up, his expression showing mixed feelings. He massaged his waistline, just above belt level.

'Well, Bob, you look cheerful, have you solved the mystery of the bank robbery?'

'You want I should reach for the

moon, Wilbur? No I haven't solved anything yet, but I've made one or two interestin' inquiries this morning. What did you have for breakfast?'

Strong dropped his spectacles on the desk and glowered at his subordinate. 'Breakfast, what sheriff could take breakfast after what happened to us yesterday? Why, if I hadn't done one or two good things years ago, the folks would have asked me for my badge, after yesterday's setback. Breakfast, huh.'

'Why don't you go along the street an' order yourself a really first rate meal? If the folks see you eatin' they'll think things are poppin' round this office, and they'll leave you alone to get on with your business.'

'It'll be a whole lot worse when they find out I haven't a clue where the money went, Bob. So maybe I ought to continue starvin' myself.'

Bob shrugged and paced about for a while, his thumbs stuck in his gun belt. 'Stop lookin' on the black side of things, amigo, an' treat your stomach to a feed. I'll hold the fort for a while. Go on, before you think about it.'

For a few seconds, it looked as though Strong would stick to his original plan, but something in the back of Bob's eye made him change his mind and ease himself out of the chair, chuckling rather grimly as he made for the door with his recently-ventilated hat.

He paused and glanced at himself in the mirror, which was screwed to the wall near the door. 'Hey, maybe the folks won't notice I've got a shoulder burn padded under this shirt, an' a knee that's almost too swollen for my denims. Okay, so I'll eat. An' we'll see how you make out as an office holder. If you get too fed up with sittin' around take a look at the reward dodgers. The faces of some of those jaspers are an education to look at.'

Wilbur touched his hat and moved outside. Bob grinned after him and tried the head man's chair for size. He was still toying with the idea of looking over the reward notices when a knock came to the door. The sheriff's office had a customer.

He called: 'Come right on in,' in a voice two tones lower than his normal one, and then as an afterthought, he picked up a newspaper and buried his head inside it.

The man who had knocked came inside, having been invited. His first words revealed that he had not seen the sheriff leaving.

'Good day to you, sheriff. I wonder if you could spare me a minute or two?'

The voice was that of Jerry Lester. Bob's heart thumped with sudden excitement. Here was his chance to get even with this self-assured young man who had beaten him in a close contest, due to a dirty move. He cleared his throat, stood up carefully, still holding the paper in front of his face, and moved towards the newcomer.

He knew enough about the office at this time to know that Lester was standing about a yard away from the stove, a pot-bellied affair with the usual long dirty chimney above it.

Not wanting to take too much of an advantage, Bob murmured: 'Now then, young fellow, what was it you wanted?'

This little speech ensured that Lester would be facing him at the moment when he dropped the paper and revealed his identity. Bob licked his lips, and let go of his screen. Lester's facial expression appeared to broaden with amazement. He had scarcely reacted when Bob's swinging right hander cracked him accurately on the point of the jaw and sent him backwards into the stove, the top of which dug into his back.

Lester groaned, straightened up and shot forward again, propelled by the sudden shooting pain in his back. The after effects of the punch on the chin made him go into a crouch, but not before a straight left had connected with his midriff and sent him back once again. This time, most of the air had been jerked out of his lungs, and it was all he could do to keep his senses.

He used the stove to support his back, and slipped slowly down in front of it until he was in a sitting position on the floor. Rex Patrick came in just at that moment.

The tension went out of Bob, who nodded to him. 'The sheriff's gone to get his breakfast, Rex. If you'd like to join him over a cup of coffee, I'm sure you know where to find him.'

Patrick looked at the fallen man, then at Bob, and finally at Lester again. He murmured something, nodded and backed out into the street, moving slightly quicker than when he had entered.

'You'll soon make a name for yourself as a peace officer, if you treat all your clients like that,' Lester murmured painfully.

'Don't you dare complain, Lester,' Bob warned him. 'You deserved a good hiding after the way you behaved in my room last night! By the way, what did you come here for?'

Lester, whose breathing was slowly easing, managed a grin. 'As a matter of fact, all I came to say was that the painting I lost had been found. Maybe you'll be kind enough to pass on the message to your Boss, if you haven't done so already?'

'Sure you didn't want to tell the sheriff his new assistant had stolen your property?' Bob suggested.

Lester rose to his feet, massaging his back and glancing sharply at the fall of dirt which his weight had shaken loose from the stove pipe. 'Aw, jest tell it the way I said it a few minutes ago, huh? After all, who wants a picture of the outside of a bank, right now?'

Bob did not answer, but allowed his visitor to withdraw on that utterance. He was thinking that no one would particularly want a picture of a bank's outside at this stage, but that certain parties might have been interested a short while ago.

9

When Wilbur Strong came back from the eating house, he was still in a restless frame of mind, and in a mood to keep away from the more influential of the townsfolk. The shooting up at the outcrop had undermined his morale. At a time when he ought to have been consolidating work started by Deputy Patrick, he had been found wanting. Moreover, he was lucky to get away with his life.

Sheriff and senior deputy prowled the room, finding it hard to settle in one place. 'Is it true you've been tradin' punches with that young painter in here, Bob?' Strong got out, at last. 'Surely I don't have to tell you that a county sheriff's office ain't the place for a brawl or a punch-up?'

'Sure, I didn't hold back when I got the chance to take a rise out of that painter fellow, but when you've heard all the facts I don't think you'll be all that put out.'

Bob turned rather pointedly on Patrick and gave him a savage glare. 'I can see you and I are goin' to get along together real fine, Rex. Couldn't wait to tell Wilbur exactly what you'd seen, could you?'

'That's enough of that, Bob. We have to have some discipline in this office,' Strong pointed out. 'He did right to tell me how he found the place. So why don't you get around to that explanation you spoke of.'

'Yer, well that's another thing. I'd like the explanation to be for your ears only at the outset, Wilbur. Why don't I go along to the livery an' run out our two horses, huh? We could take a short ride while we discuss these details I've picked up, an' the townsfolk will think we're good an' busy!'

Strong shot a rather guilty look in Patrick's direction, but he decided quite firmly in favour of the ride. Office work never really suited him. It was only when he wanted to hide himself that he found it desirable to stay indoors. Besides, he had always thought the McCleave boy was rather bright, and he might have some sort of a notion which had escaped the regular team of peace officers.

'All right, then, provided your information is relevant, Bob. Go get the horses. I'll wait here. Meantime, Rex, get along to the telegraph office an' see if anyone's tryin' to get in touch with us. An' hurry it up. Suddenly I'm out of patience.'

Five minutes was sufficient time for the sheriff and deputy to be mounted up and riding away. The telegraph clerk had nothing startling in the way of information for the county office. Strong put the rowels to his horse and headed south, intent upon riding round the town's perimeter track in an anti-clockwise direction. Bob soon sided him, and while the sheriff's eyes were busy with details connected with passers-by and buildings, Bob poured out to him the story of Lester's visit to his hotel room the previous night.

Strong became absorbed in the narrative, occasionally failing to observe a greeting from some old acquaintance who was keen to be acknowledged. 'An' this young hombre actually stood on your bare foot while he hit you, Bob? No wonder you gave him the father and mother of a pastin' when he came into the office this mornin'. Must have fairly shaken that stove pipe, too. I don't figure it's been cleaned out since before last fall. I'm beginnin' to think this young painter fellow has a special place in your thoughts. Say, maybe he does merit a little further investigation, seein' as how his paintin' of the bank turned up all that way out of town. You think that was significant, Bob?'

Bob nodded, but when the loud noises of the main creek had ceased to interfere with their conversation, he had changed to a new topic, the subject of which was the missing painting which had hung on the bank wall.

'Another painting missin'?' Strong's voice echoed disbelief. 'I did hear tell once that paintings by famous artists were likely to fetch high prices, but who would stop long enough to steal one off the wall of a bank when there were all those lovely currency notes waitin' to be picked up?'

The sheriff sounded baffled. His bewilderment grew, rather than diminished when Bob pointed out how unlikely it was that the painting had been removed at the same time as the money. 'It was removed by someone for whom it had special value. An' that's another mystery. I thought maybe I might go and ask the opinion of Jerry Lester. He might know something about the value of portrait paintings, after all.'

The sheriff started to chuckle.

'You surely do have your nerve, Bob, askin' that young fellow's professional opinion after thumping him half conscious in a peace office. It wouldn't surprise me if he protested as soon as you went near him. I reckon the army taught you a few things about fisticuffs, an' no mistake. Besides, you don't know his whereabouts, unless you have other things still to reveal.'

Bob chuckled. He patted the dun's mane before answering. 'Oh, I think I know where I can find him, sheriff. He's up at the Devere house doing a portrait of the daughter.'

The young man turned and enjoyed the look of intense surprise upon the face of his companion.

'Kind of movin' in high society, ain't he, Bob?'

'I guess you could say that, Wilbur, withour fear of contradiction. Maybe I ought to break off on this ride an' see if I can find him before the portrait is finished. He might have more to say if he was tryin' to impress one of the Deveres.'

'Any idea where he sleeps of a night, Bob?'

'None at all,' the deputy confessed,

'but I have a feelin' that he could be awfully difficult to trace, if he once got it into his head he did not want to be seen. I feel this, even though it was only a short time ago when he visited your office. Maybe I ought to make tracks for the Devere residence right away.'

Although Sheriff Strong was enjoying the company and the ride, he agreed at once and the riders parted.

* * *

There was a white painted wicker fence all around the front of the Devere residence. Bob, who had never before approached it on horseback, had to dismount a few yards short of the front gate. Obviously, no one ever rode a horse through it, or used the fence as an obstacle to be leapt over.

An elderly negro with close-cropped white hair came down the path from the house so as to meet him at the gate before he entered.

'Good day, sir, there's a big gate and

a hitchin' rail around the back of the house for anyone who truly has business with the Devere family. Folks on horseback ain't supposed to come in by this way.'

Bob grinned at the anxious fellow. 'Thanks for the information, amigo. Maybe I'll see you round the back, eh?'

The servant backed off and smiled, but stayed near the gate until he was quite sure that the young deputy would not take any liberties round the front. The gardens at either side of the house were extensive. When Bob finally reached the big gate at the back, he found a padlock on it. Moreover, the hitching rail was within the grounds. Smarting a little, he backed off his horse, mounted up, and sent it against the big gate.

In the last few paces it gathered itself together, and sailed over with six inches to spare. A white American with a lined face and a leather apron across his body darted back to avoid the horse as it landed squarely in the path within.

'I would have unlocked the gate for you, sir, if you'd waited a little longer,' the man said, with forced good manners.

'County peace officers are busy men, amigo. Besides you knew I was comin'. Who is at home?'

'Mrs Devere is in residence, and her daughter is about, too, but I don't think either of them will want to see you. What is the nature of your business?'

'Private business concerning an acquaintance of both the ladies mentioned. Be good enough to tell them that Bob McCleave would like to speak to them.' This far, Bob had tried to match the hired man for manners. But he had to spoil himself by adding: 'An' hurry it up a little.'

The man in the apron gave him the kind of look which suggested that if they met in a dark alley things would be different, but he went away, entering the house by the rear entrance. Of the coloured man there was no sign. No one appeared inquisitively at the windows. To pass the time, the visitor hitched his mount to the gate itself, and slackened the saddle.

The hired man called to him from the back door, but he ignored the summons. The man came nearer. 'You're to go round the front, Mrs Devere has your message, but don't think she's goin' to give you a lot of her time 'cause she ain't, an' that's for sure.'

'How long is it since you saw the inside of a cell?' Bob enquired mildly.

He saw by the expression on the other's face that his shot-in-the-dark remark had gone near to the truth.

'I don't have to answer that,' the fellow answered bluntly.

Bob nodded, and rounded the end of the building, sniffing the fragrance of the flowers as he went. Old man Devere, he supposed, was abroad on one of his frequent buying and selling missions. He was often away. Maybe the women had a right to be bored in his absence.

Dolores was stretched out full length on the swinging settee, exactly where she had been the time before when Bob had seen her through the glass. This time, however, she had on a pair of men's tailored trousers. She was apparently reading a glossy magazine published in Philadelphia. As she read, she was nibbling peaches. The glance she gave Bob was a very cursory one, and then she was back, reading avidly.

'If you have anything to say, young man, kindly address your remarks to me.'

Mrs Devere was again besporting herself with her usual quiet activities on the gallery of the first floor. She had the knack of wearing a look of boredom which comes easy to the faces of women of quality, particularly when those faces have been ravaged to some extent by time and high living.

Bob noted the eroded depressions round her eyes. For a moment, he felt sorry for the woman.

'Madam, I came here looking for a man who is known to you both. I wanted to consult him, ask his expert opinion on a matter connected with art.'

He noted at this juncture a slight stir of interest in both women, though neither made the slightest attempt to move into a position to eye the other.

'I'm referring to a young man named Jerry Lester, who until recently was engaged in painting a portrait of your daughter, Mrs Devere. Tell me, is Lester around? Is he expected?'

Dolores shot him a shrewd glance from under her heavy eyelids. Mrs Devere answered in the grandest manner possible.

'If there has been such a person on these premises, then he has gone, and I tell you he is not expected to return. In any case, a residence of the type of Mr Devere's is not the place for any county official to meet and exchange views with strangers. I'll bid you good day.'

The older woman's back was turned away from him that moment forward, but Bob did not mind as much as she thought. He declined to offer his thanks, knowing that his silence would puzzle the woman. For upwards of a minute, his attention was fully and frankly upon the daughter down below. Dolores had tossed aside her magazine. She had risen to her knees, almost to her feet and given him a look which made him sure that she was deeply unsettled. It was almost as if she was imploring him to do something.

She stretched out a hand towards him, but at the same time the older woman cleared her throat, and that was sufficient to make the daughter contain herself. With reluctance, Dolores took her attention away from the visitor and buried her nose in the magazine, which she was not reading.

Thinking hard about this phenomenon, Bob withdrew. He found the dun exactly where he had left it. As the gate was still padlocked, he left in the manner in which he had arrived.

10

Until mid-afternoon the staff of the sheriff's office was kept busy with routine chores connected with communications and small matters which had to be dealt with in town.

Patrick had spent a lot of the morning dealing with a telegraph communication from the next county which had come in late. In order to furnish the required information he had to sift through many documents including reward notices, and the gist of his findings went into two long telegraph messages which he took along personally to the telegraph office.

He was still away at the telegraph office when Strong returned from his late midday meal and found Bob squatting on the bench outside the office.

'Anything new?' the older man asked.

Bob shook his head. 'Nothing important, Wilbur. I gather from casual messages that the Diamond M is still managing to get along without me. No more strikes against the freight wagons. I think they're beginnin' to think in terms of doin' without me indefinitely.'

The sheriff sat down. 'But you ain't bored workin' for me, are you Bob? After all, I have given you plenty of rope to look into things in your own way. By the way, you didn't say what happened when you were at the Devere place. Maybe something that happened there is buggin' you?'

'Jerry Lester has been there, as I told you, but he's moved. Neither Mrs Devere nor Dolores wanted to tell me where. The old woman was very offhand, but I had the feeling the girl would have liked to say more, given the opportunity.'

'You think there was something between the girl an' the painter?'

'Oh, yes, I saw enough through my glass to be sure they weren't indifferent to each other, Wilbur.'

'An' now the fellow's moved on, in a hurry, if you have your facts right. Certainly if he's pulled out this quickly it looks suspicious. Are you aimin' to visit the house again when the old woman isn't there? I don't figure she comes out of the grounds very often these days.'

'Dolores does some ridin' though. They have a stable,' Bob pointed out. 'I thought the girl looked desperate enough to go lookin' for the painter. That is, if she knows where he's gone. I'd like to keep a watch on her movements for a while, if that's okay by you.'

Strong gestured with his hand. 'We ain't makin' any headway in any other direction, Bob. So have a try. Only thing is, you mustn't go upsettin' the Deveres, if you can help it.'

'I'll try not to do that,' Bob promised. 'Is it all right if I prowl the town now for a while?'

Strong dismissed him, and he moved

off with the intention of visiting the marshal's office.

★   ★   ★

In the hour before sunset, Bob commenced his vigil in the trees below the Devere residence. As the light faded, the glass became of less use to him. He had seen enough, however, in daylight to assure himself that Dolores was restless and moving about. She visited first one flower garden and then another.

By moving his position a few yards to one side, he saw a lamp burning in the stable. The man with the leather apron was in there, doing something with one of the horses. From time to time he glanced out of a small window, as though he was bored with whatever he was doing.

After a time, he came out, as though he was finished for the night, and made his way to the rear of the house. A good ten minutes went by. Only one faint light showed on the upper floor. When the figure slipped out into the open, Bob almost missed it because the person in question kept to the shadows.

He blinked and watched again, and presently the figure moved from behind a bush in the general direction of the stable. All he could make out was a big grey stetson, a shirt of the same colour, and denims and half boots. He began to wonder if there were other men in the household, other than the ones he knew about. This person did not move like either of the servants.

The lamp in the stable began to throw shadows. A faint sound of horse movements preceded the emergence of a sorrel mare, held at the head by the person seen earlier. Instead of going to the big gate at the rear of the establishment, which was on the opposite side of the buildings to Bob, the mare was led directly through the lawns on the right hand side of the building towards the small gate, where his entry on horseback had been challenged.

Bob hurriedly moved his dun back, behind the tree which had sheltered him earlier. He held it by the muzzle to keep it quiet and watched as the gate was carefully opened and used by the silent figure. As soon as the gate was closed again, the person in trail garb mounted up. The mare snickered and the pair came forward. The presence of the dun made the mare restless, but the rider did not seem to interpret the restlessness as anything to be wary of. The gap between the two persons narrowed to within ten yards, and then widened again as the mare lengthened its stride and started off down the hill.

Bob sniffed the air. He smiled. Unmistakably, the rider had left behind a whiff of expensive perfume. Either it was a man wearing perfume, or it was a woman. He figured it for a woman, and he thought that he was in luck in catching the woman secretly leaving the house in this fashion.

The town was quiet outside the amusement centre, and this made the pursuit rather difficult in the early stages. The Devere rider was in a very edgy mood, and looked back quite often to see if she was being followed.

She came away from the west side of town, and followed the line of the broad creek which had given the town its name. That particular track was one which was well used in daylight, but at that time of night no one was about. Bob had to drop back until nearly a furlong separated them. He was finding the watching and listening something of a strain on his faculties, but he kept going, and within a half hour he had the satisfaction of hearing the mare's hooves drumming gently across Broad Creek Bridge.

Beyond the bridge, the trail led eventually to the town of Oakwood, which was quite a distance further west: too far for a young woman to undertake the journey alone in the middle of the night.

Bob hurried as far as the bridge and then waited, not wanting to give away his presence by making noises crossing the trestles. Five minutes was as long as he dared delay. Then he moved forward again, quite assured in his mind that the rider had gone directly south.

He speeded up a little and that was almost his undoing, for a horseshoe struck a spark on rock a little way off the lesser track and much closer than he had anticipated. He swung to the ground and walked the dun into long grass, feeling that the mysterious rider was dismounted and keeping a watch for him.

No one else came along, and eventually the first rider's patience gave out. The mare emerged once more on trail, and the dun resumed in the rear. The pursuit continued for perhaps two more miles. Towards the end of it, the track, which had been almost imperceptible, deepened again. It was heading along the bottom of a shallow draw, and instinct alone made Bob think that humans were not far off.

Acting upon impulse, he dismounted

and began to walk the dun forward. Once he thought he saw a glimmer of light coming through distant trees, but he was not sure. The mare had stopped going forward again, and that had to mean something. Bob sighted a rock with a tree beside it. He secured the dun to the tree, and walked on, on foot.

Within a few yards he saw the glimmer of light again, but there were people between him and the source of the light.

The mare moved forward again, only to be stopped within five yards. The rider gasped, and leaned over the animal's neck. Right there in front of them was another figure which had materialized without warning.

'Who, who is it?' Dolores Devere asked, breathing with some difficulty.

The other person gave a cold, hard chuckle. 'I live with Jerry Lester. That surprises you, doesn't it? An' you don't fool me with that man's outfit on you. This is as far as you go, miss!'

The speaker was a young woman.

Her voice was not altogether unpleasant, although she was talking with a touch of bitterness. Bob moved a little closer, availing himself of some fern and small scrub cover. The one who had intervened was also dressed in a man's trail garb, and it seemed to suit her better than the girl on the mare.

'Who are you to be orderin' me about?' Dolores protested. 'I didn't come to see you, whoever you are! Now, get out of my way. I've come some distance an' I don't have the time to parley with you!'

The girl on foot chuckled. She held onto the reins, and Dolores was not able to pull away. The mare jerked its neck and snickered unhappily. Dolores' hat started to come off her head. She grabbed at it and caught it, but not before her long tresses had spilled out from under it.

'Jerry Lester always had a soft spot for a nice talkin' young woman with plenty of blonde hair and curves in the right places, but I told you you ain't goin' to see him tonight, an' I meant it!'

Dolores appeared to be fumbling around for a weapon, but the situation changed when an ominous click came from the other girl's right hand.

'You know what this is, Miss High and Mighty?'

'Sure enough. It's a revolver, but you wouldn't dare fire it at me. You don't have the nerve! So let me go, why don't you, I never did any harm to you!'

The pulling and the tugging was repeated in spite of the revolver threat. Bob was very doubtful what the outcome would be. Obviously there was no one else near enough to intervene, other than himself. He wondered if the young woman would carry out her threat, or if the gun was empty.

'Understand this, miss, an' listen real good, Jerry Lester is not for the likes of you! There's more to him than you're ever likely to find out about. Lands sakes, I'm doin' you a favour in turnin' you back. Now, will you go back to town and get in that padded bed of yours before I lose my temper?'

The struggle continued. Within a couple of minutes both women were gasping, and Dolores was half way out of the saddle. At last, the guardian of the draw lashed out with a short riding whip. She caught the mare across the rump with it and made it whinny in pain.

The animal tore the reins free from the girl's restraining grasp but not before another half dozen blows had showered upon the beast from a variety of angles. The mare pivoted on its hind legs and suddenly lunged away in the direction from which it had come.

Its rough treatment had at least assured that it would make a good speed for a furlong or so, and that it was not likely to come back in the same direction. Dolores was almost weeping with anger when she swept past the spot where the dun was tethered.

'Let that be a lesson to you, you spoiled hussy! You might live in a big house, but this is my territory an' no woman comes here unless I say so!'

The victor was standing in the middle of the path, hands on hips, breathing hard and shouting defiance at the rider on the retreating mare. In the darkness, Bob could not do other than admire her. He wished he could get closer and see the features of the woman who so intrigued him. Already he had discarded one idea. He was not hurrying back to town in the wake of Dolores Devere, even though it might have proved interesting to provide her with a shoulder to cry on.

As far as he was concerned, Dolores had served her purpose. She had shown him the way to Jerry Lester's hideout, and that really was something to enthuse over.

The girl was the first to move. She turned on her heel and stalked off in the direction of the light.

11

Bob stayed right where he was for several minutes. He had witnessed quite a lot and he was not yet ready to reveal his presence to the Lester menage. He had just about made up his mind to untie the dun and move further into the draw where the light was coming from when he heard the voice of the man in whom he was interested.

'Melissa, what in tarnation are you up to?'

It was a good strong voice, and, mingling as it did with the midnight sounds of a remote valley, it sounded even stronger.

'Melissa!'

Again, the girl failed to answer, but her steady footfalls could be heard going gradually nearer to the location of the cabin. Walking at the dun's head, Bob was soon in a position to see

Lester's shadowy figure standing near the open door of the shack, which was about a hundred yards further ahead.

'If you really want to know what I've been doin' I've been guardin' you while you slept, you fool!'

The girl's voice carried with equal clarity. She was within twenty yards of the building now, but she had slowed up, as though her efforts had lost their purpose.

'You've jest turned somebody away!' Lester accused. 'I heard the horse goin' off! Do you think I like bein' shut off here in the back of nowhere?'

'Be your age, Jerry! You know as well as I do that your life is not blameless! You have to take care, don't you?'

Bob stopped his forward progress as the other pair came together just a few feet outside the shack. They faced each other, both people of a spirited nature.

'It was the girl, wasn't it? Dolores, the one I painted in Broad Creek! Why did you have to turn her away? What harm would it have done for her to meet me here at the shack? Can you answer me that?'

Their voices were unrestrained, as they thought there were no other persons in that neck of the woods.

'You know as well as I do what trouble could have been caused if that spoiled girl took too close an interest in this shack! She must have been here before while I was away, otherwise she would not have known where to come, especially in the dark!'

Lester reached out and smacked the girl's face. She raised her hand to the place which was smarting. She gasped, and for a moment she was out of words of admonishment. The young artist swung away from her, and then abruptly faced her again.

'I know what's with you, Melissa, you're jealous of every girl who ever takes a look at me, an' that's a fact! You can't deny it, can you?'

'Damn you, Jerry, you know your own weaknesses as well as I do. Any pretty face can make a fool of you, an' that's a fact! Anybody would think you lead a blameless life the way you carry on! If you aren't real careful the day won't be far off when the two of us have to part, an' that's a fact! I can't always be around to cover up for you!'

Lester raised his hand as though to strike the girl again, but she ducked under his arm and ran into the cabin. An attempt was made to slam the door, but Lester blocked the solid wooden structure with his forearm and heaved it open again.

For almost a minute, no sounds came out of the building, and then the slamming about started again. Both voices were raised in anger. There was the sound of some furniture or boarding of some sort being thrown around. After another minute the girl gave a sharp cry, and the draw became ominously quiet.

Bob crept nearer, carefully holding onto the dun. At this juncture, he was as interested in the girl as in Lester, and the treatment which had been meted out to her had incensed him. Obviously there was some strong tie between the two, but what the girl had done seemed to have wounded Lester's pride.

Presently, Lester's shadow began to show again. He was moving around, as though clearing things away, or packing up. Bob guessed that there was about to be a break between the two. It was a good guess. After about five minutes, Lester emerged into the open carrying a saddle and a bedroll. He walked around the rear of the building, and began to saddle up.

Bob waited again, beyond the area lighted by the lamp. He shifted his weight from one foot to the other, and marvelled at the patience exhibited by the dun.

Lester had mounted up. He walked his horse, a grey stallion, into the lamplight spilling from the open door of the cabin. For a few seconds, he leaned to one side, peering indoors, but he had no last message, and this disappointed Bob, because he wanted another lead without having to work too hard to get it.

At last Lester clicked his tongue. He dug in the rowels and sent the grey forward. By the way it moved, it had plenty of bottom, and, of course, it was much fresher than the dun, which had brought Bob the several miles from Broad Creek.

The grey had perhaps moved fifty yards away from the dwelling when the girl called out from within. 'Jerry! Jerry, where are you goin'?'

The receding figure had heard the question all right, but he was still in a bad mood. All he offered by way of reply was a rude mouth noise which gave a brief echo before it faded.

Keeping at a certain distance so as not to give away his presence prematurely, Bob moved through the valley at the head of the dun. He knew that he ought to be following Lester, but the magnetism of the girl in the cabin was holding him back a little. He wanted to see her revealed in the light, so that he could see the true shape of her, and know her colouring. But any holding back now, and he would almost certainly lose contact with Lester.

Horse and man were moving at a very slow pace when the girl suddenly emerged. She had removed her hat, and between her lips was the stub of a cigar, which Bob supposed that Lester had left behind. She took a long draw at the weed, blew some of the smoke down her nostrils and dropped the butt under her boot.

Standing where she did, she was fully illuminated by the shack lamp. By comparison, she could not see anything of the angry young man who had just withdrawn from her presence.

She was younger than Lester, being possibly no more than twenty-one. Her denims looked to be moulded to her legs, which were shapely. The dark shirt, which Bob would have said was black, was now revealed as being dark green in colour. Pleated pockets on either breast failed to conceal the wearer's femininity.

The face was finely contoured, with high cheekbones. After the recent emotional scene the expression looked a trifle hard. The eyes Bob guessed to be green, although he could not tell why at the time. The whole of her head was encompassed in a magnificent bell of copper-coloured hair which had a fine sheen, and which hung straight down to shoulder length from a central parting.

During the exchanges with the Devere girl, the tresses had been tied back at the nape of the neck with a ribbon, but this had been lost during the struggle in the shack.

Bob studied the girl, almost open-mouthed. He had not seen so much beauty revealed in many a long month. The observation of Dolores Devere had not remained in his memory. Had he thought about it at that moment, he would have dismissed the Devere heiress as being too pretty for words.

Melissa suddenly stretched herself.

She stared hard, up into the night sky, seeing only stars at great distances. She arched her back, thrust up her arms and gradually spread them until they were almost out horizontally on either side of her body. Then, unpredictably, she yawned. It was a huge yawn for a woman with rather delicate features, and it faded upon the night air like a sighing breeze.

At length, the shoulders of the girl slumped. She gazed down at the earth beneath her feet and slowly trudged back indoors.

Bob blinked after she had gone. He realized that the vision of her had almost mesmerized him. Moreover, her presence had so held his attention that Jerry Lester had put many useful yards between them. Yards which might mean that he would give his pursuer the slip.

He murmured to the dun: 'Come on, Blaze, follow that grey. We can't afford to lose touch.'

It was clear that Lester would be a much more difficult subject to follow unnoticed than a girl who was unused to night riding. Bob trailed him, keeping well to the rear. In a way, the dun's tiredness helped. It meant that they were unlikely to go blundering into the rear of the mounted man up ahead, unless Lester stopped.

A little over an hour passed, and Bob was beginning to slump over in the saddle, when it became clear that Lester was not going back to Broad Creek. He had turned away to westward well short of the bridge over the creek which led to the county seat.

The trail the two riders now followed was up and down in varying grades, but always south of the running waters of the creek.

Inevitably, the strain of riding by night, and keeping his movements a secret, began to take a toll of Bob. Another hour passed with the geography of the land to westward making a hazy jumble in his head. He was too tired to think it all out. Without being in the least aware of it, his eyelids closed and the forward progress was kept up solely by the dun, which reduced its rate of progress a little more, but did not give up.

The time came when the sparkling waters of a spring crossed the trail and this had the effect of bringing the dun to a standstill. It had its long neck craned over, slaking its thirst when Bob gradually recovered himself and found that he had been murmuring the name of the girl, Melissa. For another minute, he remained stiff and straight in the saddle, seeing again the vision of her as she had been outside the shack, just before he rode away.

Thoughts of her, and her relationship with Jerry Lester tantalized him. Was this remarkable woman his wife? Obviously she had lived with him, and that seemed to suggest such a relationship.

He murmured: 'Melissa Lester.'

Swinging to the ground, he crouched down and swished the spring water around his tired face. Sleeping alone in a cabin, miles away from anywhere meant that a woman had spirit. Not that he doubted such a thing, having witnessed the exchanges with the Devere girl and then Lester.

He found that he was more curious about Melissa, more drawn to her than he had been to anyone of the opposite sex that he could remember. Perhaps the attraction she had for him would lead to trouble. Certainly it could if she was Lester's wife. But did married couples quarrel and fight and part like this couple had done?

Whatever Lester thought of her, he had left her there on her own, to fend for herself. For the first time, it occurred to Bob that he did not know for certain whether in fact the girl was alone in the shack. But surely no one, old or young, could have cowered away indoors while that terrible row was going on without making some sound or sign?

He rolled over onto his back, and yawned rather satisfyingly. This at once reminded him of how the girl had yawned. The memory of her was astonishingly fresh, but he had to get on. How long he had slept, he did not know. He was not even sure that Lester was still ahead of him, although he would have gambled on it. Dawn was still some hours away, but he knew instinctively that he was heading towards the west. And in that direction there was only one community of any size in the area. A town known as Oakwood. In size it did not differ very much from Broad Creek, but its local wealth in the past had come from silver and copper mines, whereas the county seat had prospered through livestock reared nearby.

If Lester was headed for another out of the way shack, then he had made his escape, and the only possible way of getting in touch again would be through the girl, Melissa. That prospect did not displease, but Bob thought it was fairly safe to assume that Lester had gone to Oakwood, or somewhere close to the thriving town.

Even though the trail was cold, he would ride to Oakwood and take a look around. Who could tell, he might find Jerry Lester there painting a picture of another bank!

This thought made Bob chuckle at first, but later he treated the notion more seriously. He began to see this line of investigation as being a lengthy one timewise. Especially if he failed to locate Lester in Oakwood and had to try and trace him through the girl.

One thing Bob was clear about at this stage. He *was* following his own inclinations. He was doing what he wanted to do, and the feeling of initiative was breeding confidence in him. He thought he might do Wilbur Strong's office a whole lot of good before he was through.

12

When the dawn broke, Bob was stretched out on a bench a few yards along the first thoroughfare he came across in the sleeping town of Oakwood. He had tethered the dun with its saddle slackened to a rail a few yards away which gave it access to a water trough.

Quite a fair spell of time elapsed before the sun's slanting rays came over the top of the buildings opposite and started to warm one half of his body. The sensation was sufficient to rouse him. He sat up, knuckled his eyes and peered up the street, looking for signs of life. Only two dogs and a cat were abroad at that time of the morning, and animals did not offer him much consolation in the way of company.

He stared down at the deputy's star pinned to his shirt, and wondered what good it would do to be worn in the town of Oakwood. In looking for Lester, was he, he asked himself, acting on his own behalf, or was the investigation really a sheriff's office matter? For a time, at least, he decided to take it down. He would mingle with the local people as an ordinary traveller.

First of all, he took the dun to a livery at the other end of the street. One man was awake and working there. All the time Bob was asking about a friend who painted pictures, the stable hand listened gravely and sucked at the stem of a corn cob pipe.

At length, he explained: 'Can't say I have much time off from this job, stranger. Can't say I know anybody who has the time to paint pictures, either. You'd best ask questions some place else.'

In a Chinese restaurant, Bob ordered and ate a large plateful of ham and eggs. When he had washed it down with a liberal amount of coffee, he enquired of the Asiatic proprietor if he knew of a young man who had recently come to town who painted buildings. The restaurant owner politely shook his head, and this he did again when Bob's description of Lester failed to create any interest.

One customer inside the restaurant, and another one about to enter both answered in a negative fashion, and Bob began to feel that he had taken on quite a task. Lester might not even be in the town at all. And if he didn't set up an easel, there was a good chance that he might remain unnoticed, even as a visiting stranger.

There were four main thoroughfares in the town. One after another, Bob explored them. Half way down Second Avenue, he thought he recognized the back of an acquaintance. He hurried forward, but when he arrived at the location of the empty shop, or office, the figure had vanished.

The elusive figure had definitely not been that of Lester. Bob had taken in for the silhouette of Wilson Hargrove, the insurer. In the few seconds when the figure was there ahead of him, the deputy had received a definite impression of a frockcoat, a derby hat and long black hair with a few grey ones at the sides.

The door of the empty shop was open for anyone to walk in, but there was no private property in it. Someone had stirred the old dust, and there were footprints in the dust up the alleyway beside the shop. At the rear of the alley were the usual rather unsightly backs, strewn with garbage, stones and other items.

The nearest human was a bald man in a white overall sweeping dust out of the rear entrance of a saloon in the next street. Bob wandered back into Second Avenue and further scrutinized both sidewalks. He supposed it was possible for a man who lacked sleep to imagine he had seen someone he was looking for, but at the time he had been searching for Lester, not Hargrove! So was it possible he was imagining things?

He doubted it very seriously. Hargrove had to be about in one of these towns in Rockwall County. Why not Oakwood? And why shouldn't he be on the point of setting up in an empty shop?

The shop next door was a barber's. Bob spent a half hour in there, having a shave and a haircut, and questioning the Mexican hairdresser about the next shop and the man who owned it. This led to a contact in a mercantile store, but no definite knowledge that a man had acquired the key of the shop, or a lease on the property.

Long before noon, Bob's patience began to give out. He walked along to the town marshal's office and there made the acquaintance of the Siddons brothers, Mark and Nathan. Mark was the town marshal, and Nathan was his chief deputy. They were dark-eyed and swarthy, with a slight suggestion in their countenances of mixed blood. Mark had a neatly-trimmed black moustache of the drooping variety, and eyes which revealed a very positive nature.

When Bob had talked himself out, Mark coughed, spat tobacco into a garbage can, and recapped.

'Now tell me if I've got this right. You came along here following up the trail of a young hombre who painted a picture of a bank in Broad Creek. The same bank that was robbed, huh? An' you were followin' him because you thought he might have been able to answer questions about another painting which was found to be stolen after the robbery. Am I right about that?'

Bob nodded.

Nathan, the younger, cleanshaven brother added: 'An' this far you ain't spotted him anywheres in town?'

'That's about the size of things, gents. So if you do come across a man called Lester, who answers the description I gave you jest now, maybe you'd be kind enough to get in touch with Wilbur Strong's office at the county seat?'

'Sure enough, we'll be glad to do that,' the town marshal replied warmly. 'But do I take it that you'll be leavin' town real soon, jest havin' got here?'

'I reckon I'll have to do that, marshal, on account of I might lose touch with another contact in a cabin situated out of town.'

The Siddons brothers kept their faces as bleak as poker players, but it was fairly obvious that they thought Bob was haring around the county to no particular purpose. He was about to say that Lester might be completely innocent of any crime connected with the bank robbery in Broad Creek, but he thought better of making such a statement.

Instead, he thanked the peace officers for their patient co-operation and got as far as the door. There he hesitated, until Nathan asked if there was anything else.

'One other man I'm interested in. I thought I saw him in Second Avenue a while back. Name of Wilson Hargrove, an insurer of other people's goods. Did you hear tell of such a man recently arrived from the county seat, or anyone setting up afresh in that sort of business?'

'Never a whisper, Bob, but we sure will keep our ears open as long as you assure us it's important!'

The marshal came as far as the door and courteously shook hands before returning to his chair and the conversation with his brother.

No progress on all fronts, Bob was thinking as he made his way to the telegraph office. There was really not much to keep him in Oakwood unless it was to stay there indefinitely waiting for his man to show up. He entered the office, exchanged the time of day with the clerk, and slowly composed a message for Wilbur Strong.

It read as follows: —

To County Sheriff, Broad Creek.

Interested party moved to this area. Send news of any new developments. Also present whereabouts of W. Hargrove.

Bob McCleave,
Oakwood.

The clerk rapidly assessed the value of the message and named a figure. As Bob parted with the money, the clerk appraised him afresh, guessing at his official capacity on account of the way in which he addressed the sheriff.

'Send it as soon as you can, please. I'll be back to take the reply when I've had a meal.'

Ninety minutes later Bob came back for his reply, which had been waiting for him for quite a time.

Bob McCleave, Oakwood.

No new developments here. Present whereabouts Hargrove not known. Keep in touch if not planning early return.

County Sheriff, Broad Creek.

Bob left with the message screwed up in his pocket. He was still restless, even in the heat of the day. And having failed to keep track of Jerry Lester he was doubly anxious to retrace his steps to the cabin where the girl, Melissa, was to be found.

The dun was reluctant to leave town but when it became aware that Bob was determined upon another big effort, it stopped protesting and plodded out of town on the east side, retracing its route of the night before.

The trail was a little busier now, and many people in wagons and on horseback were drawn into the side of the route to rest until the most punishing hours of the sun were over. Bob insisted on a steady, economic pace which kept the miles rolling by and the cabin in the draw coming gradually nearer.

A big wagon went by with two young women outriders. The sight of them made Bob wonder how he would feel if the girl he sought had already left the shack. What would he do after that? Could he justify staying away from the county seat any longer? He doubted if he could. Thoughts along these lines tortured his tired brain for a while, until he had to put them aside or lose confidence in his protracted search.

The joint needs of the dun and himself made him pause for a spell and bathe in a shallow backwater connected with the big creek. After a time, he felt refreshed and the dun recommenced its journey with renewed vigour and confidence.

Bob kept it on the south side of the trail and coaxed it to find its route of the previous night. The direct route to the trestle bridge was on a down gradient. As they joined two wagons, a buckboard, and half a dozen horse riders on the downward stretch, Bob felt that they had missed the turn-off to Lester's shack, but fifty yards from the lowest level the dun sidestepped through other horses and jerked its neck in the direction of the ill-marked turning which led into the southbound track.

Bob's spirits surged, although it seemed quite different from the route taken at dark. Every now and again, he closed his eyes, or half-closed them and attempted to relive the route of the night before. A great weight left his mind when he recognized the tree and the stone by which he had left the dun earlier.

There were several hours of daylight ahead this time, and even if the girl had gone it might be possible to pick up a few clues as to Lester's true mission in life from things they had left behind in the cabin. All the same, the rider hoped that it would not come to that.

He reined in at the spot where the struggle had taken place between Dolores and Melissa. Only the upper half of the cabin was in sight from there. He drank from his canteen, and decided to make the dun wait a little longer for a thirst-quenching drink. Almost certainly there would be a pump at the back of the dwelling.

Now that he was close, he experienced a feeling of shyness. He had to go and talk with the girl, and explain how he came to be where he was. If she was in the prickly mood of the previous night, perhaps he would not get the chance to question her. He recollected that she talked of protecting Lester. Perhaps it would be better to invent an excuse for the visit, avoiding any hints of the truth, which might make her stay silent.

Through the trees, he started to work out possible theories to cover his presence, but none of them sounded particularly convincing. For a time he was practically counting the trees as they went by, and then he was in the open and just short of the shack. There was no sign of life. Not even a chicken scurried away as they approached.

The dun came to a halt unbidden and turned its neck towards its master.

'Okay, Blaze, you did a good job. So take it easy now.'

He swung out of leather, stamped his boots for a moment on the solid earth and then turned his attention to the saddle. As he loosened the cinch and rocked the saddle, he called: 'Anyone at home?'

No answer. He figured as much. The spirited young woman of the night before would have been out before this, with or without a gun, to see who was prowling around. He had a feeling of anti-climax. No need for hurry now, although he was very curious indeed to know more about the dwelling and its recent occupants.

He pointed the dun towards the grassed hollow in the rear of the building and slapped it across the rump. It went willingly enough, and he lost interest in it for the time being.

The door was open. Inside, he found a wooden floor had been laid, although the boards were worn. Against one wall was a double bunk. Old and discarded clothing, mostly men's, hung on nails hammered into the walls. There were two tables: one in the middle was used for meals, and a second one had pots and pans stacked on it, and a washing up bowl.

At the far end of the one large room a curtain hid a low single bed. A crude wooden ladder with eight rungs on it led up to an open loft which was half the length of the building. Odd glimpses of the loft's contents suggested that it was used as a repository for suitcases and pieces of equipment not in everyday use.

Bob noted all this, and the fact that the building had two windows both containing all the necessary glass, but after that his observation did not get beyond the scattering of painter's canvasses which were leaning against the walls at floor level.

Seeing them, he started to whistle to himself. The painting of the bank which had first brought Bob into contact with Lester was still rolled up on the second table, but it was the framed ones which took the visitor's eye.

About four of them were landscapes of good quality. Another showed cattle in a stampede. A sixth showed a number of cow ponies fretting inside a rope corral. But it was the last one which really held Bob's attention and set him thinking. This was undoubtedly the missing portrait of the founder of the South-Western National chain of banks, Jonathan Beauclerc.

Bob knelt before it and checked the details as he had remembered it, and as it had been described to him. The short brows, the winged collar, the lined face and the piercing grey eyes. It was all there, down to the details of the suit. In the bottom right hand corner of the canvas was a signature. The sort of scrawl put on the canvas by the artist, after it was finished.

Bob murmured aloud: 'J. Beauclerc. Now there's a strange thing.'

A voice so startled him that he almost rose from his knees to his feet, but the ominous click of the revolver prevented him from doing a thing so foolhardy.

'All right, cowboy, so you've had a good look round the art gallery, an' now it's time to leave. So on your feet, but make your move real slow, 'cause bein' a woman I'm a trifle nervous with a long-barrelled gun like this in my hand.'

Bob cleared his throat. He said: 'I don't figure you for the nervous type of woman, Melissa.'

As he stood up, still moving with great caution, he had the satisfaction of hearing her gasp.

13

Melissa was stretched out full length in the loft, with her head and shoulders just showing over the edge. Her two hands were out of sight, but the muzzle of the Colt just showed. It was trained on his back.

'Turn around, stranger!'

Bob was smiling as he carried out the order, and his apparent self-assurance had the effect of riling the girl with the gun. He stared at her and went a little way towards demoralizing her. He could see at once that his guess about the colour of her eyes was right. They were very green, and at this time they mirrored the doubts she felt about him and his reasons for being where he was, uninvited.

'Who told you my name, stranger?'

'Oh, it was Jerry. He was shouting at the time. I couldn't help overhearing it.'

Melissa moved a little closer, taking the gun in one hand. With her free hand she touched herself as women often do when a little in doubt. Her fingers explored her throat.

She said: 'You've been to this place before. Did he bring you?'

Bob shook his head. 'Did he hurt you, I mean when you had that row?'

Again the free hand was busy. It explored the ribs beneath the shirt, as though the green cloth hid bruises. He could see by the slight change of her expression that she knew that he had been in the draw the previous night.

'It's none of your business whether he did or not, mister. Now keep your hands up an' move a little further away. You hear me? I'm comin' down an' I don't want to land on top of you.'

Bob grinned a little more broadly, but he did move back about another yard. He was enjoying himself rather a lot. His outlook still had the girl baffled, but she was making an effort to sound as if she had everything under control.

Moving with the fluidity of a cat, she came slowly to her feet. One mocassined foot was extended until it found a rung of the ladder. She swung slowly through the air until all her weight was on the rung. Her next move took him by surprise. She turned sideways, still holding the gun in his direction and heaved the ladder out of the vertical.

It swung away from the loft and executed a nice arc, coming to a halt when one of her feet hit the floorboards. She remained upright, lowered the ladder away from her, and surveyed him from the new level.

'Unstrap that gun, an' do it real carefully.'

Bob lowered his hands rather gingerly. He began to fumble with the buckle, but his eyes were still on the girl.

'You sounded much more formidable when you were sounding off at Dolores Devere.'

The generous lips tightened. She knew now for sure that he had been

184

near during the night. He knew Jerry and he knew the Devere girl. Who was he, this mysterious interloper? What right had he to come uninvited, in this way?

'Did Jerry ever ask you to come here?'

Bob shook his head again. 'I did want to talk to him, though, and he moved out of town in such a hurry.'

Shrugging slightly, he dropped his gun belt on the boards and gestured towards the nearest wooden stool, as though he wanted to sit down. Melissa jerked the gun muzzle at him and asked another question.

'Who are you, an' what's your business? You'll allow a girl has to ask things like this when a total stranger walks into her home and starts examinin' things.'

'You don't have anything to panic about, Melissa. After all, wouldn't any Westerner have walked in when there was no answer to his call? An' wouldn't any man have taken a close look at the paintings you have around the walls? After all, it ain't often a man walks into a cabin so full of talent!'

By her expression, Melissa approved of the talk of talent, but she was still very impatient for some answers. So impatient, in fact, that she stepped forward and ran her hands over the outside of Bob's pockets. The star concealed in the shirt pocket revealed its shape to her hand.

'Uh-huh, a peace officer,' the girl murmured. Her pretty mouth turned down a little at the corners. This discovery of course made a difference. It always did, whether the discoverer was law-abiding or otherwise.

Bob fished in his pocket and tossed out the star, which landed on the table in the centre of the room. 'Deputy Sheriff Bob McCleave, workin' out of the county sheriff's office, Broad Creek. Until a short while ago, I was an officer, in the army, cavalry to be exact.'

Melissa was interested, but at the same time rather concerned about the peace officer tag. 'You'd best sit down. Take a stool.' She walked away and laid the revolver down on the table, sitting on the far side of it from her visitor.

'I think you went to a great deal of trouble to find this place, an' if I can believe you, simply to talk to Jerry. Now, what can a peace officer want with a rovin' painter?'

'He did a painting of the bank in Broad Creek. Everybody in town knows that. I wanted to ask him about another painting. One which was lately discovered missing from the bank. Off the wall of the bank, in fact. Jerry being the only painter I know, I came looking for him. I followed the girl Devere who seems to have a crush on him. Was that so bad?'

Melissa's shoulders moved in a gentle shrug. 'What about the painting you say is missing?'

'Well, why don't *you* tell *me*? It's standing over there against the wall. That's the one of the old man, with the subject's name painted in the corner.

How about clearin' up this little mystery? You could be doin' Jerry a big favour.'

The girl writhed on her chair. She looked as if she wanted to explain it away forever, but the explanation, she knew, would have to be a good one. As the seconds went by, it became clear to Bob that she did not want to divulge the truth.

'How do you know this painting is the one you are lookin' for? There might be two — '

'It isn't likely, and I'm sure you know that as well as I do. I saw it myself, a year or two back. And I've had it described to me. The subject is the founder of the bank, you see! There's hardly any room for error.'

To Bob's great surprise, his interrogator suddenly appeared to be in the grip of strong emotion. He watched the tears well up in her eyes, and the effort she had to make to blink them away. Her shoulders shook, and he waited before asking anything further.

'I — I don't think I can answer that

to your satisfaction, Mr McCleave. All I can say is that Jerry has more right to that picture than any man living. I hope you'll believe me, but the nature of your work, I fear, won't let you leave the matter there.'

Bob felt around for a smoke. The girl indicated a tobacco sack on a wall shelf, which he collected. He rolled a smoke and achieved some satisfaction from the taste of it.

'I don't think the recovery of that painting is a vital matter,' he observed. 'Certainly nobody sent me out to look for it. I wanted to ask Jerry about it because I thought there might be a tie up with the bank robbery. You see how it is?'

Melissa nodded. She tucked her hands between her knees and seemed to be at a loss for words. Her restless eyes viewed every article of furniture in the building, avoiding Bob's face for as long as possible. She was staring out of the back window when she broke the silence.

'Well, all I can say is that Jerry ain't here, an' I don't have any idea when he'll be back, if ever.'

'Do you think he's in trouble?' Bob queried lightly.

'He's a headstrong young man, sure, he could be in trouble. Who can keep him out of it? But this far no cell has held him for very long. I'm certain sure there's more good than bad in him. I wish I could say more.'

Bob also wished he could say things which would take away from the girl the load of worry she obviously felt on Lester's behalf. But since he had entered the cabin, the discovery of the missing bank painting had further complicated the Lester business. He felt that his further investigations could only heap more troubles on her young shoulders.

In the midst of a growing silence, distant horse movements could be heard. At once the girl tensed up, and grabbed for the gun which was on the table. Bob rose to his feet, wondering what she expected and how he was likely to come out of the next meeting, if the two of them were involved.

He said: 'Are you expectin' visitors? Is that what all the fuss has been about?'

Melissa had tensed up again. 'Let's put it this way. I'm not keen to be visited right now. Maybe they ain't headin' this way. They seem to be comin' from the north, or the north-east.'

'You want to take a look at them before they get here?'

With just a few seconds of hesitation, Melissa nodded. Bob offered to go along with her, so that she was spared the embarrassment of having to give him orders again at gun point. He preceded her out of the door, went into a crouch and ran for the trees which had screened him on the way in. She had to run fast to keep near him, but when she overtook him, she found that he had leapt for the lowest branch of a tree, in order to get up higher. She had the gun, but the initiative was not hers.

In a very short space of time, Bob was stretched along a branch, breathing heavily. He was weaving his neck this way and that to catch glimpses of the distant riders through the foliage.

'It's difficult to see them through the leaves,' he called out, 'but there are several riders an' they appear to be comin' this way. I can see the horses better than the men.'

'Describe them, an' hurry it up, pronto!'

Obviously, the girl was anticipating trouble. Bob did his best to get the required information and to get it quickly.

'I see a black stallion forked by a man in a dark outfit. An' there's a pinto following up close. Rider on its back kind of shortish! Does any of this make sense to you? I think they're comin' here!'

'It sure does make sense, so get down, an' don't delay! You have to do exactly as I tell you from here on in, an' there's no time to lose! So jump!'

Bob made his leap. He had scarcely straightened up when the Colt dug him in the back. One glance into Melissa's face showed that she was really frightened of the outcome of the next meeting. He went ahead of her, and she ran into the cabin behind him.

'Grab that badge, an' anything else that will show you've been here. An' come round the back! Hear me?'

Bob nodded. The girl recoiled from him when he touched her on the shoulder as he went out again. At the rear of the building they ran towards the cropping dun, and pulled up, one on either side of it. Melissa's distress was beginning to communicate itself to Bob. He had his gun belt in his hand, but she did not suggest he should buckle it on.

'Quick, out of this hollow an' into the next one further over. It's deeper and ringed with trees. Get the dun into it as soon as ever you can.'

'Are you plannin' on staying away from the cabin, Melissa?' Bob asked, rather breathlessly.

'Jest keep on goin' right ahead. Don't pause till you're over the high ground an' down the next dip!'

All the way up the slope of the hollow, the runners felt the tension and the sounds of the steady advance of the latest-comers carried to them. At last they were over the rim and dipping down beyond it. The down gradient was steep, and their legs reacted to the change.

Nearing the bottom, Bob slowed to a walk, and Melissa did the same, keeping behind him.

'Say, Melissa, shouldn't you give me an idea what this is all about?' Bob protested.

Before the girl could answer they heard the first shout of the new arrivals at the shack. The newcomers knew her name and they were bandying it about as though they were not used to be kept waiting. Bob peered back up the slope and wondered if he might have to defend this frightened girl from some special peril.

'What is Jerry Lester to you?' he asked irrelevently.

'My brother, of course. An' remember this, in bringing you out here I've done you the father an' mother of a big service today. You remember that if you ever meet up with Jerry again. Jest don't ever forget!'

Bob turned to face Melissa, but before he had the time to do it properly, the Colt which she had been nursing connected with his skull. His senses left him.

14

Melissa stuck her gun in the waistband of her denims and walked away from the fallen figure of Bob McCleave with a show of reluctance. She had not enjoyed having to cut him down with the butt of her revolver, but the way in which her life was suddenly becoming complicated left her with little alternative.

Obviously, she could not allow a head-on showdown between a decent young peace officer and the bunch of wild riders who were calling out for her at the cabin. She reflected that since she had left the family's permanent home, she had never known the sort of security which most young women of her age took for granted.

'Melissa! Where in tarnation are you hidin' out? Can you hear me?'

'Yes, of course, Crease! I'm coming,

so take it easy, will you?'

She sounded aggravated and that was intentional. The coming interview was going to be a difficult one. One which she would have liked to avoid, had it been possible. As she came up the slope of the lesser hollow at the back of the cabin, a face appeared at the rear window. She had been spotted.

The face was that of Shorty Pawson, a restless young rider with short legs and a big nose which he often poked into other people's business. He shouted: 'Here she comes, Slim! It's okay!'

Three other men, already dismounted and in the dwelling, crowded to the door to feast their eyes upon the girl as she came into view. She knew them as Brad Leamer, Dandy Lamont and Jinx Denville. A fifth man was still mounted on a spirited black stallion. He answered to the name of Slim Crease.

Crease had a flattish face. His dark shirt and pants were offset to some extent by a white bandanna, a touch of brightness at the throat. He was just turned forty; over six feet in height, and he wore twin .44 revolvers low on his thighs. The hardware gave a hint of his chosen profession.

'Come along, come along, Melissa, you've known me long enough to know I'm an impatient man! Hidin' away don't do any good with the likes of hombres such as I deal with!'

He was rigid in the saddle, controlling the restless black with powerful wrist and arm work.

'I wasn't hidin' from you,' the girl retorted, 'why should I have to hide, anyway? I didn't know you were comin'!'

Leamer's round pockmarked face rounded still more with admiration at the way she stood up for herself, in the face of the leader. Dandy Lamont, a fine dresser in a lace-trimmed shirt, a leather vest and a Texas-rolled hat, perhaps admired her more than any of the others. He had decided that if ever he got the chance Melissa Lester was going to be *his* girl. Jinx Denville, a decade older, distinguished by an eyebrow scar, black eyes, and a goatee beard, likened her to horse flesh. He thought she was the likeliest looking filly he had seen in many a long month.

'There's questions I have to ask you, Melissa,' Crease called out brusquely. 'Where have you been?'

'Out for a walk, Slim, so don't get so steamed up. This neck of the woods gets kind of lonesome at times. If you want to know any more, you better dismount an' come inside.'

Melissa headed straight for the door, her green eyes flashing. At the very last moment, the three men clustered there backed out of her way. Inside the hut, Shorty Pawson sniggered at her from the other side of the bigger table.

'Howdy, Shorty, are you as childish as ever? Want to play games with me, do you?'

Pawson moved in behind her, but in so doing he was in the way when she swung the heavy coffee pot which had been standing on the stove. He backed off with some of the wind knocked out of him, and a lot of the cockiness.

He would have advanced against her, had not Lamont and Denville held him back. The tension remained at a high pitch until Crease walked into the building and at once took the attention of everyone. He sat down at the table and waved a long forefinger in the girl's direction.

'Now see here, girl, quit playing around with the eating utensils and give me your attention. Where's Jerry?'

The girl ran her fingers and thumbs through her hair, and retied it at the nape of her neck with ribbon. She sat down at the table, and clasped her hands and faced Crease with determination reflected in the tautness of her mouth and jaw.

'I don't rightly know where he is. We had a tiff an' he left. That was last night. Do you have to see him in a hurry?'

Crease stood up suddenly, overturning the stool he had been sitting on. 'I have to keep track of all and sundry in between jobs. Of course I have to see him in a hurry! He should have been here, an' that's for sure. I'll bet he ain't done a darned thing since the last job!'

As though to prove the point, Crease gave his attention to the paintings standing against the walls. He picked them up and threw then down, one after another, as though they were of no consequence. Melissa rose slowly to her feet, her hands gripping the table edge rather tightly.

'If you don't know it, every one of those paintings took hours an' hours to do. Ordinary people the likes of you an' me, we couldn't do that sort of work, even if we wanted to! So go easy on them, will you? You don't have to destroy them?'

Crease paused in his endeavours. He was deliberately goading the girl, and getting some enjoyment out of doing it. His henchmen, all four, were scattered about the room, relaxing in their own different ways, and studying the clash of personalities.

Crease grinned at them in turn. He picked up the painting of Jonathan Beauclerc, frowned at it as though it meant something special and then shrugged. He dropped it, broke the fall with the toe of his boot, and left it where it came to rest.

He walked back to the table and stuck his boot up on the corner of it. His size dwarfed the girl, but she tried not to show what his pose was doing to her confidence. Her mind was busy with a few untruths which might or might not rid her of the present menace.

Crease remarked: 'I never could understand why the Boss put so much trust in a painter! Fancy havin' a painter in *our* line of business. Glory be, it don't bear thinkin' about. Now, see here, Melissa, you've always been pretty close to that brother of yours. *I* know it, even if you've never admitted it. So you have to have an idea about where he's gone. A shrewd idea. So tell me what you think!'

Melissa met his eyes, but she was in no hurry to answer him. Meanwhile, the coffee pot began to bubble. Brad Leamer, who ate more than most, went over to the second table where he found a few biscuits. He tossed one on the table in the middle. Crease moved quickly and caught it. He broke it with the fingers of one hand, and filled his mouth with it.

Melissa said calmly: 'Oakwood. If you want my advice — '

'I make the decisions,' Crease cut in. 'You jest give out with the facts.'

'If you keep interrupting, you'll have to wait longer,' the girl pointed out, shrugging her hair against her neck. 'I was about to say that he will have gone to Oakwood to contact the Boss. But you don't want my advice, so that's all I can say.'

'What else could you have said, if you hadn't been put out?' Crease queried lightly.

Melissa studied her nails. She made no attempt to answer. This seemed like an opportunity for Shorty to get his own back. He went up behind her with his belt knife in his hand and gently rubbed the point of it against the nape of her neck. The girl shuddered, stiffened and half rose to her feet.

Crease gave Shorty an urgent signal to desist. When she had seated herself again, it was seen that she had a small carving knife in her hand which had been in the drawer in front of her. Watched by his friends, Shorty swallowed hard and moved back against the nearest wall. He was perspiring, and the others enjoyed his discomfiture.

'There's nothing to keep you active boys here. You ought to ride for Oakwood right away. There's another job been set up.'

This revelation loosened the tongues of the listeners. One intimated that they had not had their cut of the last one.

Denville remarked: 'She wants rid of us, Crease, don't take no notice of her. I reckon we could all be comfortable here tonight.'

Pawson was smiling again, and Lamont appeared to be secretly pleased. Leamer said: 'Maybe there's something or someone she don't want us to see.' He sniffed, but did not bother to glance at her face to note the reaction.

'How come you know about the setting up of a new job?' Crease demanded to know.

'I'm not permitted to say. You'll have to ask the Boss as soon as you see him. I want all of you to remember that I told Crease to ride to a rendezvous with the boys without delay.'

No one dared to give more than a slightly perceptible nod. Nor did they hasten to break the silence in the cabin. But Crease was impressed. He knew from experience that this was the time to set up a new job. He would also have gambled that the next important place in their plans would be Oakwood. He had few doubts about what he had heard.

'All right, then, we'll take a meal here an' then we'll hit the trail for Oakwood.

You don't know exactly where the rendezvous is likely to be?'

Melissa stood up. Already she was feeling a little better, more secure. 'Nope. I couldn't really say exactly where it will be. After all, I'm only a woman. There's a limit to what the Boss would want me to know.'

Crease nodded, and moved towards the cooking stove. He was hungry and he did not mind who knew about the emptiness of his stomach now that he had talked and made his plans for the immediate future. He was an easier man to deal with. Whatever his faults, he kept to a plan. Knowing this, Melissa knew that the hours of her present ordeal were limited.

★ ★ ★

The two senior members of a family of jays were squabbling and flying round their nest on the far side of the hollow where Bob had spent his unconscious period. He watched them for a while, as his head and his stomach seemed better for the lack of movement.

The dun was aware of his returned senses, but it made no sort of demands on him in case he got up in a hurry and wanted to be carried a long way. It had cropped all the way round him without disturbing him. It might almost have been in cahoots with the talented but unpredictable Melissa.

He thought about her again. He knew she was under a lot of stress, but he had not thought it was sufficient for her to put him out of action with a revolver butt. He thought there was something undignified about being rendered unconscious by a woman. Certainly it was not the sort of thing a young peace officer recounted to his partners around the office stove in the depths of winter. It was a thing to forget.

Anger began to bubble up inside of him. He had known two Lesters and both of them had robbed him of his senses after taking an unfair advantage of him. It would serve her right if he treated her the way he did her brother, except that she was a girl and he could never take that sort of advantage of a woman. However, knowing that they were brother and sister, and not any other sort of special relationship he felt a warm feeling radiate through him, in spite of his head pain.

Who had she been protecting most when she hit him over the head? Had it been herself, or him? Perhaps it was both of them. As she knew full well he was a peace officer, he thought a fair conclusion about the latest arrivals was that they were law-breakers. Otherwise, why put out of action a peace officer?

Bob's interest was warming. The Beauclerc painting did tie in Jerry Lester with the bank job, and as he had bank robbers on his mind at this time, it was interesting to think that these feared riders might be members of such a renegade team.

Where did that leave Melissa? In a grave position, at the very least. If Jerry, and this crowd of riders were all in the raiders gang, she could hardly come out of the business with a clean reputation for honesty. At that moment, it gave him little comfort to feel that he was the only peace officer who knew anything against her.

His attitude to his job, at which he was comparatively new, was likely to change, strictly on account of one pretty girl . . .

He sat up, rubbed his head and fetched the almost empty water canteen from the dun's back. He drank some and used more of it to dab his face and head. Presently, he felt better. He had no clear idea of how much time had passed since Melissa went away.

He felt, though, that it was time he disciplined himself to do something about the present state of affairs. No one had been near his hiding place. Therefore, he could assume that no one knew about his presence other than the girl. He left the dun right where it was, collected and strapped on his gun belt and wriggled up the slope with his spyglass to hand.

At the rim of the hollow, he was very cautious, training the glass through the long grass which grew thickly there. The lesser hollow had acquired five more horses. The black stallion and the pinto, which he had seen before, and also a bay, a roan and a claybank. All good looking horses with plenty of bottom, but seemingly happy to be resting.

It was not possible to get around the hollow without one or other of them becoming aware of his presence, so he did away with his plan to crawl closer and contented himself with a prolonged observation from where he was.

Every now and again, sounds came from the shack. Sounds of raucous laughter. The kind associated with food and drink rather than the more brutal kind which Bob feared for the girl. For the present, he felt sure that she was in no personal danger.

He would bide his time, and probably make a decision like he had already done recently: to stay with the girl, or track the departing visitors.

15

An hour after sunrise the following morning, a low-barrelled piebald and a sweat-streaked grey stallion were stepping side by side down a narrow swale in a south-easterly direction from Oakwood. For upwards of ten minutes there had been absolute silence between the riders, although they had been riding since before sunrise and were well known to each other.

The nostrils of Jerry Lester flared from time to time, while Wilson Hargrove's bleak countenance was still suffused with colour occasioned by recent anger.

The piebald sidestepped and this annoyed the grey, and the quarrel between their riders started up all over again.

'Jerry, it ain't no use beatin' about the bush! I've said the New Mexico

Territorial Banking Company is the one for us to hit in Oakwood, an' you won't have it at any price. If you've offered me one reason against it, you mentioned six. Let's face it, you ain't really in favour of my kind of business. Why, if I hadn't had a slight hold over you concernin' some currency notes that weren't printed in the normal fashion you'd never have worked for me at all, even though you do appear to have a down on the South-Western National Bank which you want to keep to yourself!

'I ain't happy about our association any more. An' there's that sister of yours, too. She knows far more than is good for her to know. I'm beginning to rue the day I took the Lesters into my confidence, an' that's a fact.'

Jerry gave Hargrove a half minute in which to cool down, and then tried to placate him: 'Boss, human relationships never stay the same indefinitely. I'm sorry ours seems to have changed for the worst. There was a time when it suited your purpose to use the shack I share with Melissa as a place to go to earth.'

Hargrove had suddenly become alert. 'Quit talkin',' he growled, 'it's times like these when out of town riders like us get themselves in trouble! I'm pretty darned sure we're observed by men in that thicket fifty yards ahead, on the right!'

Hargrove was right about their being observed, but for once he was about to encounter friends.

The voice of Slim Crease called out: 'Howdy, Boss, this is a good a place as any for a rendezvous. Come on over, we're jest about to take breakfast!'

Hargrove grinned and coughed on phlegm. He dug his heels into the flanks of the piebald and went ahead of Lester, into the thicket. Lester gave the assembled five desperadoes all a bold smile, but their reactions were cool towards him.

'We visited your sister, painter,' Denville remarked.

He saw the sudden look of apprehension fill the back of Lester's eyes, but the young painter checked his fears and did not ask after Melissa. Crease was wearing his usual poker expression, but Jerry did not think that his sister could have been roughed up on this trip. But now, he bitterly regretted the precipitate way in which he had left her to fend for herself, following the fracas over Dolores Devere.

Within five minutes, all seven of them were eating bacon and beans fried by Brad Leamer, who ate more than the rest, and therefore found it convenient to be cook. A fallen log and two big rocks provided seating accommodation for Crease, three of his buddies and Hargrove. Leamer did his eating on his feet, while Jerry ate off the ground.

Inevitably the masticating jaws gradually worked slower and gave up. Coffee followed, and then tobacco, and presently the important talk began.

'How was it at the cabin?' Hargrove asked.

'All right, Boss,' Crease explained slowly. 'Melissa appeared to have done all we asked of her. But I found something which disturbed me a little. I was examining the paintings at the time. Then I found one which was rather special. A portrait of the founder of the South-Western National banks. A man named J. Beauclerc.'

Hargrove massaged his back-sliding nose and tugged on his moustache.

'How did it get there?' he asked abruptly.

Crease nodded in Jerry's direction. The latter flinched, but made no attempt to deny the charge. A growing wave of hostility spread among the assembled outlaws. Until this time, Crease had kept to himself what he had found out back at the cabin. Denville, Pawson, Leamer and Lamont stared at each other as a glimmering of the truth dawned upon them.

'That old man's painting hung in the Broad Creek branch of the South-Western until such time as it was

216

removed from the wall without our knowledge! A highly dangerous proceeding, you'll allow, Boss, an' one which might have brought a posse hot on our trail at a time when we least needed it!'

Jerry Lester threw down his battered eating plate. 'All right, I took the painting. I can see now that it was a silly thing to do, but I never meant any harm. I — I jest fancied it, that's all. An' well, no harm has been done. Nobody, other than Crease, here, has been bright enough to know that it was missin'. So what have you lost, an' why all the long faces?'

Lester glared at each man in turn, but no one was inclined to answer him. It was the turn of the Boss, and he was taking his time, toying with a small cigar, making his victim squirm.

'Boy, if you don't know about the risks you've taken you shouldn't ever be ridin' with men. You've run the risk of jeopardizin' the whole outfit, an' that ain't nice. It means the likes of us can't really trust you, in case you spot something else you fancy, something you'll steal an' not tell us about. An' you might have been picked up by the law before we ever made our strike, seein' you sneaked into the bank before the raid. Am I right?'

Reluctantly, Lester nodded. Some of the gathering had a certain kind of respect for a loner who could make it into a bank single-handed and steal a painting and get out again, still undetected. But none of them dared to show any sympathy at this time. It was not the time to side with a minority of one. Quite the contrary.

'So what are you plannin' to do with me?' Jerry queried.

Hargrove shrugged. Instead of answering, he dipped inside a huge pocket of his coat and pulled out a big wad of currency notes. They were all made up into bundles, and the bundles were then held together by a big band. It was pay day. The faces of the conspirators showed pleasurable anticipation.

Crease received the first wad, thrown into his lap. Then Leamer, Lamont, Denville and Pawson, in that order. There was a brief moment of hesitation, and then the last packet was tossed across to Lester. He was in a mood to reject it, but he knew that any move which would rile up the gang would do him harm in the immediate future.

He breathed more easily, thinking that if they intended to do away with him, they would not have paid out his wages. Hargrove allowed him to think that way. It suited his purpose, for a short time.

* * *

Half an hour later, the group broke camp, mounted up and set off in the direction of Oakwood once more. Hargrove and Denville were in front, talking together. Pawson and Leamer came next, and then a trio, Crease, Lester and Lamont. Lester was just ahead of the other two, and riding in the middle.

For a time, Lester was apprehensive about Crease riding so close, but the latter appeared to be completely relaxed. He was riding without his gauntlets, which was unusual for him. Very soon, the unused track they were riding along would run out into the well-used trail between Broad Creek and Oakwood.

As soon as that point was reached, Lester could feel certain that no decision had been taken to remove him. The pay-out had boosted his confidence a little, but he was not certain that he had been forgiven his past misdemeanours.

Some fifteen minutes later, a fissure opened up beside the track. Hargrove appeared to rein in and act as though the snare was a nuisance. He rubbed out his cigarette butt on his saddle horn and tossed it over his shoulder. As soon as this was done, Crease edged closer to Lester and hit him across the back of his head with a gauntlet loaded with sandy soil. Lester's senses reeled, and Lamont, who was in position on the other side to catch him, did so.

Almost ten minutes had elapsed before Lester was conscious and thinking clearly again. By that time, he had been lowered thirty feet into the bottom of the fissure. His hands, arms and legs had been well trussed, and a gag had been tied across his mouth. Crease climbed out of the mouth of the fissure and glanced down at him, grinning broadly.

'Farewell, buzzard bait,' he called. 'If it's any consolation to you, the birds of prey won't peck your pay, we've borrowed it back again. Adios, painter, I guess you'll do some good canvases in the next world, eh?'

The group thought it was unlucky to tote along with them the mount of a man they had left for dead. Being superstitious, they took the grey about a furlong from the fissure, and got rid of the saddle. Another furlong further westward, they released the unwanted animal, driving it by shouts and curses into a tangle of scrub.

That, as far as they were concerned, was the end of the Lester affair.

Bob McCleave, who had taken a grave chance over what was intended in regard to Jerry Lester, stood over the fissure about fifteen minutes after the armed gang had left. When he saw the plight Jerry was left in, he talked to the dun as he would have explained the situation to a human.

Leaving the lariat attached to his saddle horn, he went over the lip of the fissure holding on to the other end.

'Brother, you sure are crazy to have anything to do with hombres as mean as that outfit.'

Bob was bent over Lester, fumbling with the fastening of the gag, which had been left too tight and would possibly have suffocated the wearer in time. When the relief came, Lester's breathing was loud and noisy for a time, but he started to recover gradually from that time forward.

A knife parted the rope bonds, and within five minutes, Jerry stood up, supported by his deliverer.

Bob, who was perspiring through his efforts and the heat in the fissure, remarked: 'You know what? It ain't healthy for a peace officer to do all his work single-handed. In order to untie you, I've had to let Hargrove an' his boys go on alone. As like as not I may not find them again before it's too late.

'By the way, your sister was all right when I left her.'

Lester gripped him on hearing this, and his grasp was one of relief rather than anything else. 'You left after Crease an' the others came away?'

Bob did not know individual names for the outlaws, but he nodded, and presently he started to help the other out of the fissure. He got out himself first, and had the assistance of the dun when it came to lugging out Jerry.

As soon as the latter emerged, and sprawled out in the open, he began to feel better. Bob gave him a smoke, which he accepted gratefully.

'Painter, your sister did me a favour

back there. She said to pay it back to you, if an' when the opportunity arose. I consider the score is even from now on.'

Lester thanked him most profusely. 'If you want to get after Hargrove and the boys, I've finished with them now. I can tell you more or less what they're plannin' to do in the near future, though. They're plannin' to rob the New Mexico Territorial Banking Company's place in Oakwood.

'Usually, they take a lot of time lookin' over the place before they make the strike, but seein' the forward lookout man, namely, me, is no longer workin' for them, I'd say they'll strike without much delay this time. This afternoon, or tomorrow, at the latest. So there you have it. You must know that Hargrove is the brains behind it, and that he uses the insurer business as a front for his normal activities. More than that I can't tell you.'

'You've told me a lot, Jerry. More than I might have hoped from an ordinary renegade. If I'd been wearin' this badge I carry for much longer I've have had to take you in. As it is, I'm prepared to take a chance with you. That is, if you'll do exactly as I tell you.'

Jerry grinned. 'All right, what's the scheme?' he asked eagerly.

'I'm goin' into Oakwood to do what I can to stop this robbery an' to apprehend the gang. As for you, you're to go back to that shack of yours, collect Melissa an' clear out. An' I mean clear out! No hangin' around hopin' to see Dolores Devere, or anything like that. Out, is over the border. Know what I mean?'

'I know what you mean, amigo.' Jerry scrambled to his feet.

Bob forked the dun, and hauled in his lariat. He pointed out the direction which the riding group had taken. 'If they've turned your cayuse loose, it'll be along there some place. Take a look, by all means, but if you don't find it quickly start for the shack on foot.'

'Okay, amigo, that's good advice. Any

messages for Melissa?'

This was a shrewd query on Jerry's behalf. He saw his deliverer colour up a little. 'If there was likely to be any point to it, I'd send a message. All you can say is that I kept my promise, an' wish her well.'

They parted and Bob moved the dun at a good pace. In leaving Jerry behind he had the feeling that he was turning his back on the only possible contact with the girl. The feeling he experienced was a new and devastating one. For a time, it troubled him and kept his mind from the serious consideration of what lay ahead of him.

16

Around ten o'clock that same morning, Bob McCleave hitched his dun outside the office of Town Marshal Mark Siddons in Oakwood. He found the marshal indoors on his own and quite surprised to receive a return visit from the sheriff's representative after so short a time lag.

'Take a seat, Bob, an' spill your information,' Siddons invited. 'I can see you have plenty to say, an' it has to have a bearin' on things in this town.'

Bob sat down and relaxed. 'Can we be overheard here, Mark?'

The marshal slowly shook his head. He glanced around the room. Each of the cells which formed the rear of the office had a barred gap in their outer walls. In order to convince Bob, he walked into both empty cells and stood on the bench so as to be in a position to peer outside and be sure that no one was hanging about at the back.

'Nope. There's jest you an' me, an' the walls don't have ears. So go ahead. Get it offen your chest.'

'Mark, the New Mexico Territorial Banking Company is about due to be hit by a workmanlike bunch of raiders. The same ones who struck at the South-Western National in Broad Creek. I learned most of the details from a prisoner of theirs who was left to die in a gully.'

Siddons sniffed. 'Ain't been an attempt on a bank in this town for over three years. Still, you sound as though you know what you're talkin' about, Bob, so I'll listen real good to any details you can give me. Maybe we'll be able to put this renegade gang out of business at one go!'

'Here's hopin' we manage to pull it off, amigo,' Bob replied warmly. 'If they work accordin' to their usual plan, they'll hit the bank directly after siesta time, this afternoon or tomorrow at the same time. Although they're in the district right now, I'd say tomorrow would be the most likely time because their horses could be tired today an' they're rather keen on such details.'

'So what do you advise me to do, Bob?'

'Get in touch with the head man at the bank. Alert a few trusted men who can ride hard at short notice and shoot straight. Have them in and around the business section of town, and warn them that they might be called upon to ride at very short notice. Think you can do that?'

'I sure enough could. Why, as soon as that thirsty brother of mine shows up I'll send him round town with a list, to tell the riders to be ready.'

Bob rose to his feet. He grinned briefly. 'I'm formulatin' plans all the time, so I'll probably be back in touch real soon. Right now, I figure on visitin' the telegraph office, an' also the bank president. Could you tell me if I can locate the bank official without makin' it too obvious?'

'At his house at the west end of town, on high ground. He don't come around these days until after eleven in the morning. Wife likes his company, so he says. He's called Samuel H. Grosse. You'll find him, all right, but he might start to panic when you state the nature of your business.'

Bob thanked his colleague for the advice. He adjusted his hat and stepped outside. The dun bore him along to the other end of town. His star was in his pocket, so as not to draw attention to himself. He thought he was doing right in keeping his business a secret on this occasion. Every step the dun took, Bob's eyes were on the alert for signs of the outlaw bunch. On several occasions his glance met with curiosity from others, but he did not see any of the horses he had seen earlier, or any man who could seriously be considered as one of the raiders.

Samuel H. Grosse was sitting under a spreading ornamental tree in the front garden of his house at the west end of town. He was a rotund man with a fair quiff swept across his forehead. His cheeks were flabby and his spectacles rested rather unevenly, low on a fleshy nose.

He was rocking himself on the edge of a wicker chair, a fat prosperous man in a grey suit. His cigar burned down very slowly. It scarcely ever went into his mouth.

Sitting opposite to him was his wife. At forty, she was fifteen years his junior and rather prim. Her dark hair was piled up on the top of her head, as it had always been in her schoolmistress days.

She said: 'Samuel, I hate to disturb your reveries, dear, but there's a man coming up the path. A riding man. I thought you'd given instructions around the town not to be disturbed so early in the morning.'

'Why, why, yes, I have, dear, but perhaps this is an emergency of some sort. Perhaps I ought to hear what the fellow has to say?'

Mrs Grosse pouted in annoyance and

shrugged her shoulders. By the time Bob was close enough to talk without raising his voice she had disappeared behind a copy of an east coast newspaper.

'Mr Grosse, I'm sorry to burst in upon you like this, but my business is your business, and it is urgent. Especially from your point of view.'

'Young man, this is a private residence, but not a business office. I never conduct business at home.'

'Sir, if you'd get yourself along to your place of business it wouldn't be necessary to intrude upon your private life. Kindly ask your good lady to step indoors for a while. What I have to say may not be good for her delicate ears.'

Mrs Grosse made outraged noises. While the banker summoned up enough invective to put his visitor in his place, Bob thought of other things to say.

'I've come here straight from the town marshal's office. I'm trying to safeguard bank property, an' you aren't makin' it easy for me. I'm from the county sheriff's office.'

He flashed his badge, made a remark about the recent bank robbery in Broad Creek and began to get co-operation. The lady blanched and withdrew, and the formidable Mr Grosse offered his best attention.

★   ★   ★

At half past eleven, a wagon bearing a family going further west pulled into town and complained to the town marshal's office that they had been fired upon from a spot beside the trail about two to three miles away. A spirited return fire appeared to have made the attackers have second thoughts about holding up the wagon for money.

Bearing in mind all that Bob McCleave had said, Marshal Siddons rode out of town towards the north looking for trouble. Within half an hour he came upon another wagon which had been fired upon and his men were in time to fire off a few angry shots at the troublemakers before they withdrew through a huge patch of scrub and scattered through some ribbed and barren country.

For upwards of another hour, the mystified marshal patrolled the route coming from the north-east.

When they paused for a rest and refreshment in the hour after noon, he was asked a question which he could not answer.

The rider said: 'Mark, you ain't noted for givin' out information, but you must have some sort of an idea what sort of trouble is brewin'. So how about tellin' us? After all, every man here has taken you on trust.'

Siddons spent a long time with his bandanna, mopping his face and neck, and then giving his moustache a second going-over.

'Boys, I can't say a lot about this development on trail. It's true I had some advance information about local trouble, but it wasn't about attackin' wagons at all. So I'm in the dark. All I know is that we're on the spot, an' somebody sure is lookin' for trouble up and down this trail.'

'Do you ever get the feelin' that they're doin' it simply to draw us away from some place?' another rider queried.

Siddons winced at the suggestion. That idea had been in the back of his mind for a long time. He was thinking what a fool he would look if the bank was hit in his absence, after the warning which Bob McCleave had given. Within five minutes, he had given the order to turn south again and to keep riding at a good pace for town.

★ ★ ★

The time was a little after a quarter past two when the drooping posse riders walked their sweating mounts back into town. Marshal Siddons was twenty yards ahead and still worrying about the bank.

'How was it?' a storekeeper called out.

Siddons' face showed no signs of optimism, but then it never did, so it was best to ask about the outcome of anything serious.

'Jest so-so, mister. We fired on a few riders who were causin' trouble and sent them offen the trail, that was all. So far we know it's jest a bunch of trouble-makers out to harass the local travellers. It won't come to anything if the travellers keep their guns handy. Anything happened in town while we've been away?'

He asked the last question as casually as he could, but his thoughts were keyed up about the answer. A negative shake of the head eased his mind for a while, but the hour which followed had his nerves jumping all the while.

The bank opened as normally at three o'clock. Nothing happened. Everything was calm. No one appeared to have the building under special observation, other than the Siddons deputy. Bob stayed in his hiding place, which was close and unpleasant until three-thirty, and then he emerged and made his way out of the bank into the fresh air by way of the back entrance.

Samuel H. Grosse was almost prostrate with repressed fear by the time to close the bank came round.

After sundown, a brief council of war was held in the banker's sitting room. Such a thing had never been done before, and Mrs Grosse, although she did not show herself sufficiently long to admit it, was deeply impressed.

Bob presided over the meeting, which consisted of the banker, the two Siddons brothers, and two senior bank tellers, the bachelor brothers, Richard and Walter Bardoe. These two clerks, both in their early thirties, were tall, thin and sparely built. Richard, the older brother, wore spectacles which magnified and altered his eyes, whereas Walter had good vision and surveyed the world rather matter-of-factly through his own unaided, blue bulbous eyes.

Walter Bardoe asked the first significant question: 'If I may say, gentlemen, we're lucky to have a little more time in hand. But only if we use it well. What outside help are we going to get, if the raid occurs tomorrow?'

Bob was impressed with Bardoe. He talked with more refinement and sense than his pompous master. 'I can't rightly say, Mr Bardoe,' he replied earnestly. 'Earlier today I sent a telegraph message to my superior suggesting that we were expecting currency trouble here in Oakwood. The sheriff has sufficient intelligence to screw the truth out of such a cryptic message, but I don't know how many riders he will be able to send in this direction by the assumed time of the strike.'

'But he will try to do something positive,' Grosse persisted.

Bob talked for another few minutes, mainly to give the assembled gathering confidence in Wilbur Strong's ability and initiative. As they started to go over ground already covered, Bob's protracted efforts began to tell upon him.

He dozed off, and was left to sleep in his chair until an hour before dawn.

At that time he was called, according to his own wish, so that he could begin his preparations for the day in total darkness.

★ ★ ★

The heavy wooden cupboard which had been selected as the place for Bob's concealment in the bank was six feet high and four feet wide. It had been stripped of its movable shelves so as to give him the maximum chance of movement during the time when he had to stay hidden and observe the bank interior.

He was hatless and bootless, but his weapons, of course, were in there with him. Two rows of circular holes had been drilled in the woodwork of the doors. One of them so that he could see out easily when standing up, and the other for his use when sitting down. Several large ledgers had been stacked in the bottom of the cupboard so as to give him something on which to rest his weight.

All through the morning session, he kept his vigil but nothing happened. The shutters were closed during the midday closure in order to enable him to get out and stretch himself before the critical time. He had little appetite, but the rest, taken in the back room, did him a lot of good.

At a quarter to three he was back in his place of concealment and itching to be in touch with the desperado gang which had so dogged Rockwall County. He had plenty of time for conjecture. Apart from some details about the Lesters, only one other consideration baffled Bob. He felt certain that the murder of Curly Thomas was connected with the subsequent happenings, and all he could think of as a reason for the elimination of the fellow was some sort of connection with Wilson Hargrove. Perhaps he knew Hargrove of old, and the gang leader was afraid that he might divulge vital details while he was under the influence of liquor.

The bank wall clock was out of sight from Bob's angle. So was the outside door area. Not that this consideration worried him unduly. The Bardoes came in directly at three o'clock, closely followed by another clerk, Lance Wills, a short, stout, bald man in his middle forties. All three glanced at the cupboard, which was on the customers' side of the counter, as though to take comfort from Bob's presence.

There were guns hidden on the tellers' side of the barrier, but the clerks had been told to use their own initiative about them, in case they drew hostile fire by using them and thus endangered their own lives.

The trio became busy almost at once, lugging trays of money out of the safe. The unknown voice made its wants known exactly two minutes later.

'Howdy, gents, this is a stick-up! I'm not wearin' this white bandanna over my face jest to clean my nose, so take what I'm sayin' seriously. My friends, here, are all professionals. They know what they want, an' what to expect from you. So don't give them any trouble!

'Right now, we'll have all three of you with your hands on the counter till we get organized!'

One flash of Walter Bardoe's bulbous eyes was sufficient to get an immediate reaction. The brothers crouched and threw themselves flat on the floor behind the counter. Lance Wills was a little late in following them. For his slowness, he was untidily grooved along the side of his head from Slim Crease's right hand gun.

Crease sounded hoarse, after that. 'All right, you, Brad, an' you, Dandy, get round the back of that counter real fast an' keep a watch on the clerks, I don't like the way they reacted!'

Bob, who was leaking perspiration in his hideout, waited until the two men in question had gone through the flap and were giving their attention to the clerks.

He gave Crease time to call out something about filling the bags, and then threw open the doors, stepping out into the open and showing the intruders a pair of .45s.

'All right, you Hargrove boys, the game's up! This is your one an' only chance to drop your weapons! So take it! Hesitation could mean death!'

Crease was near the rear, as usual, and Shorty Pawson was marking the outside door. First Lamont and then Leamer cautiously showed their heads above the counter, looking to the other two for a lead. Bob fired a bullet along the top of the counter between the two heads, in order to back up his command.

This had the effect of releasing the tension in the other outlaws. Leamer's head stayed in sight. Lamont bobbed down again. Crease and Pawson were too far apart for Bob to have his eyes on both at once.

He guessed correctly that Pawson was going to fire at him first. With his right hand gun he blasted off at the short figure crouched near the door, and luckily he was on target. Shorty's bullet came right back at him at the same time. Bob felt the hot wind of it across his cheek. Pawson crouched, clutching his chest and gradually folding up.

Crease got off a snap shot which gave the deputy a shallow groove on his left shoulder. Bob knew the pain would come later, along with the stiffening. He was facing too many hostile guns to survive. Unless he made a fast move. He raced towards the door, but avoided it as three guns cracked behind him. At the last moment, he hurled himself at the big pane of glass on the right hand side of the door and went through it in a shower of chards, erupting into the open air at the same time as a vicious exchange of shots was taking place between Jinx Denville, the horse minder, and Deputy Nathan Siddons. The town jailer fired and missed twice, but Siddons, who was considered deadly behind a hand weapon, caught Denville half way along an alley opposite and drilled his chest with two lethal bullets.

The exchanges out of doors, rather than any other consideration, made Slim Crease give the orders to evacuate. He knew that in some way the authorities had had word of this particular strike, and he was anxious to get out before they were all eliminated.

Bob threw himself down in the dust, after shaking as much of the shattered glass from his body as he could. Lamont and Crease came out together. Bob's accurate shooting ended Dandy's brief career, while Siddons shot Crease through the throat.

The shooting faded, but all the men on the outside were suspicious. Brad Leamer was the only man still to come, and as the seconds rolled by and Lamont and Crease twitched their last in the dirt, it did not look as if he was coming by the front door.

Leamer took a chance. He showed himself by the huge hole in the window, made by Bob's body. With hands raised, he stepped closer. The raider aged in the few seconds it took for Bob to raise his arm and give the signal for Leamer to emerge.

Siddons, as efficient as ever, rose to his feet and collected his prisoner, while Bob dusted himself down and tried to think what was still to do.

'Anybody else waitin' round the back of that buildin' opposite?' he shouted.

'If you mean anybody with the outlaws' horses, there ain't nobody around there waitin' for the trouble you're givin' them!'

Men were beginning to appear now, but they were keeping back in case any mad dog of an outlaw would try to shoot his way clear. Bob took a long look at Siddons' prisoner after the mask had been lowered. He pointed accusingly at the fellow, as a flash of recognition took place.

'You're the jasper I winged durin' that attack on Diamond M wagons! If you don't want another hole in the belly tell me where to locate Hargrove! You hear me?'

The pockmarked face showed fear, especially when Siddons moved closer swinging a six-gun.

'I don't know where he is, mister, honest I don't!' Leamer was hoarse. Nothing would have made him lower his hands at a time like that, but he swung one hand in a high arc, as though suggesting the northern part of the town.

'Where's your brother, Nathan?'

'Coverin' the west side of town, tryin' to stop any getaway in that direction. He expected the sheriff's riders to be coverin' the east end by this time.'

'They won't be far away, you can bank on that. But the leader of this outfit is around somewhere. I know what he looks like an' I'm goin' to get him, if I can!'

Nodding briefly, Bob ran up the alley beside the bank, crossed an open space and found the dun waiting for him. It was the work of a few seconds to tighten his saddle girth and mount up. He walked the animal across the dirt and emerged into the next thoroughfare. Seventy yards of fruitless and worried searching came to an end when a crouching rider emerged from an intersection forking a piebald horse and leading a sorrel.

'Hold it, Hargrove!' Bob yelled. 'Your boys are taken, an' we know your part in what's happened!'

By way of an answer, Hargrove put the spurs to his piebald and sent it across the street towards the other side of the crossing. The piebald answered readily enough, and the sorrel went along at the same speed under protest.

Bob turned after the runaway, and almost ran into a shot fired by Hargrove on the turn. The pursuit became a chase, although the dirt underfoot did not help in the next hundred yards. At another turn, Hargrove released his spare horse and sent it back across Bob's path.

They exchanged three shots apiece

without doing any damage. As the dirt of the town street surfaces started to give out, Hargrove fired three accurate shots at the dun's feet. He so far startled it that it bucked and reared and sprang sideways, putting one hoof into a deep rut.

From this it emerged unhurt, but further behind. Bob began to see that he might have a long ride on his hands and he regretted being without his hat and boots. The stirrups began to dig into the underside of his feet. Even the dun knew the difference.

Seventy yards separated the two riders when the first clump of timber came towards them. Hargrove headed towards it with his attention on what was happening behind. The rifle bullet, fired from the trees, took him completely by surprise, and dropped him neatly on his behind in the dirt. Hargrove dropped his weapon and slowly toppled over, a sure sign that he did not have long to live. Bob overtook him quickly, then, and dismounted to be near him before the end.

'Need any more help?' the voice of Jerry Lester called from the trees.

'No thanks, Jerry. Jest carry out that last instruction I gave you before it's too late. This whole business could get too much for one sheriff's deputy if you don't clear out real soon!'

Bob had a clear impression that Jerry was pulling out, but his attention was on the fallen man. Already there was an ominous flow of blood from Hargrove's mouth corner.

'Hargrove, it's all over. You want to confess?'

The gang leader nodded gently, but couldn't find the energy to make an ordinary statement.

Bob said: 'You were the brains behind the bank raids in Broad Creek an' Oakwood?' Hargrove nodded. Bob resumed: 'An' the insurance business was jest a front?' Another nod. 'How did Thomas fit in? Did he know too much about your activities?'

Hargrove thought about that a little

longer, but then he nodded with a show of reluctance. His time was almost run out. In order to catch his last utterance, Bob had to bend closer.

'You're all the insurance your Pa needs for his wagons, Bob.'

Hargrove said this in a scarcely perceptible whisper. He died on a sigh in the throat and his head rolled on his shoulders.

17

Melissa Lester had walked a quarter of a mile from the draw where her home was built. Bob dismounted as soon as he saw her, and draped his arm around her until she discovered the several tiny cuts made by flying glass and the shallow groove on his shoulder.

'Is it all over, Bob?' she queried anxiously.

'So far as I know it is, Melissa.' He outlined what he knew of the outlaws who died, and she put names to the men as he described them. He went on: 'I nearly missed Hargrove, but Jerry was ahead of me and he shot him. I told Jerry to collect you an' clear out, but you're still here.'

'I figured we Lesters, or Beauclercs, to use our proper name, owed you explanations, Bob. Jerry's still about, but he'll still head for the border, if you insist.'

'I must insist, Melissa. You know how it is. He's helped in a bank robbery. They'd have to take him in if they knew. But you were talking about explanations.'

Melissa nodded and rested her head against Bob's good shoulder.

'Our father, Jonathan Beauclerc, was the founder of the Beauclerc Banking Company. For a time, he prospered, but then he became the victim of a conspiracy. People who had held opposing views in the Civil War worked to put him out of business. They caused a run on two branches of the bank. That did us a lot of damage. Father was worried. His doctor advised him to retire, but he wasn't willing. The worry affected mother's health. A rumour was put around that one of our ancestors was an illegal immigrant. You can imagine what it did to my folks.

'There was a fire at the family home in Pecosville. We had to move out and live in a much smaller place. Mother died of a broken heart. And finally Pa had to sell out to a man we've always supposed was one of the men who conspired against him.

'The South-Western National, which is the old Beauclerc bank, used to belong to us, so you can imagine what my brother feels like knowing someone else is reaping the profits. He was the one who painted his father's portrait, so he stole it back again when he found it quite by accident, gracing the wall of the Broad Creek branch. Do you blame him?'

'No, Melissa, I can't say that I do. Has he ever attempted to do anything fraudulent against any other group of banks?'

'Never! He's too proud, an' that's why he fell out with Hargrove over this last job. The New Mexico Territorial Bank belonged to another outfit. He wouldn't co-operate.'

'I know, I know.' The walkers paused on the edge of the trees. Bob drew Melissa into his arms and kissed her. It was a moment of great satisfaction for both. 'How would you like to put the name of Lester, and Beauclerc, behind you forever?'

'In marriage?' Melissa queried quizzically. 'If the right man asked me, it might be all right. Jest so long as my brother was at liberty an' able to go on with his painting.'

'I think he'd be all right to stay at liberty if he'd jest start hitting the trails for the border, like I told him to!'

Bob had raised his voice till he was almost shouting. He had guessed that Jerry was hidden somewhere around the building. The paintings still scattered around the floor of the shack confirmed the painter's presence. Bob and Melissa sat close on a bench, sipping coffee and talking.

'I can tell the authorities that he shot the outlaw leader before he headed for the border. Then, if he can keep away for a few months until his name has been forgotten, maybe he could come back again an' start a new life. My Pa, Arthur McCleave, would take kindly to a young man who could paint a good likeness of him. What do you think?'

'I guess he's got enough patience to do as you suggest, Bob. As for me, I'd like to jest pack a few things and then be taken into town to visit that family of yours. If they'll have me around, that is.'

The girl had turned shy, but Bob soon dealt with that. He told her that she could either be married to a deputy sheriff, or the manager and future owner of the Diamond M holdings.

'I don't mind either way,' Melissa confessed at length.

Security and love were the things she was after. Jerry, hidden in the loft, cleared his throat to show that he had heard and understood. He came out of hiding in time to help his sister and her intended to pack and start their trip.

He felt lonely for a time, but his own packing helped to distract him and soften the blow of the parting.

Other titles in the
Linford Western Library:

WARRICK'S BATTLE

Terrell L. Bowers

Haunted by the past, Paul Warrick is assailed by bad memories, and in an attempt to forget, drifts from town to town finding work. But a shoot-out at a casino lands him in jail, and with the valley on the verge of a range war, Paul's actions might be the fire to light the fuse. Paul becomes involved in the final show-down — and he must not only save his life, but also his own sanity at the same time!